Buzzard Breath

Buzzard Breath

by MARTY CRISP

SCHOLASTIC INC.

New York Toronto London Auckland Sydney

ISBN 0-590-97000-3

12 11 10 9 8 7 6 5 4 3 2 1   6 7 8 9/9 0 1/0

Printed in the U.S.A.   40

First Scholastic printing, September 1996

For all my best friends through the years: P. G. Simmons, Dorothy Miller, Trudi VanDyke, Maggie Heaney, Ellen Jones Whitesell, Evelyn Dries, and, of course, G. B. Crisp. Having any friends at all is good. Having best friends is better.

CONTENTS

Prologue

Mrs. Ludke looked like a basset hound.

Will studied the short, plump teacher with her round, wire-rimmed glasses, her brown hair tightly braided and wrapped around her head.

No.

A basset hound wasn't quite right.

He chewed thoughtfully on the eraser end of his newly sharpened yellow number 2 pencil. Mrs. Ludke had the floppy jowls of a basset, but her eyes weren't the proper sad, droopy brown.

Instead they were pale blue dots behind her glasses, like the piggy little eyes of an English bulldog.

That was it!

Will doodled a fat little bulldog in the margins

of his math work sheet. He could feel David White's eyes looking at his paper. "Move your hand, Will," David whispered urgently. "Give me a break here, pal."

The boy sitting beside him was always trying to peer over Will's shoulder and copy his answers. David was a tall, skinny fourteen-year-old, with pimples on his nose and chin. He'd been held back once in the first grade, and once more in third.

Will wished David had been held back just one more year. Then *he* wouldn't be forced to sit next to him all the way through sixth grade. But since both their names fell together in the alphabet, Will was stuck.

He would have liked David all right, despite the pimples and the copying, if the older boy didn't always make fun of him. Even though David got lots of Ds and Fs, he still acted as though he knew everything about everything. He acted as if everybody else in the class–especially Will–was just a dumb doofus.

The only time David White was nice to Will was when he wanted to copy off his paper.

Will tilted his work sheet to the left, making it harder for David to read it. He'd finished the problems quickly. Now that he had time to think, his thoughts, as usual, turned to dogs. It relaxed him to think about dogs.

Will wished he had his American Kennel Club

book with him right now so he could look up English bulldogs. But even without the book he was sure he was right about Mrs. Ludke. She looked exactly like a bulldog.

Will figured he must be almost an authority by now, after all the studying he'd done about dogs. He even knew the Latin names for all the major dog muscles: the *gluteus medius* for wagging the tail, the *scutularis* for pricking up the ears, the *biceps femoris* for putting on great bursts of speed.

Secretly he'd made up a Latin name for himself.

Will Winkle, Dog Expert would be: Canine Willibus Smartibus. Or, sometimes, when he wasn't feeling as sure of himself, he might make it Doggus Expertia More-or-Lessia.

But whatever you called him, there was no question that Will had pegged Mrs. Ludke in *her* true genus.

In fact just like a bulldog with a bone, she was standing in front of the class right now with a new student. The new kid looked scared. Probably didn't like having her paws on his shoulders, thought Will. What was she barking–saying–now?

Will shook his head to clear it of the dog images that crowded it. Beside him David was already snickering and making rude noises.

"Class, I'd like you to meet Henry Higgenbotham."

There was a surge of giggling laughter, quickly cut off when Mrs. Ludke frowned sternly and continued. "Henry and his family have just moved here from New York City." She gave the runty chubbo a reassuring pat on his shoulder and shoved him down the middle aisle between the desks. "Henry, there's an empty seat in the back row."

She looked directly at Will and gave him a warning look. "Right next to William Winkle. You won't be in alphabetical order for the time being, but you will be sitting next to one of our top scholars. Which gives me a good idea. William, why don't you be Henry's guide today? Show him around. Help him feel at home here at Notchcliff Middle School. You'll do that for us, won't you?"

Us? Who was us? The class definitely didn't care if this kid felt at home or not. Even Mrs. Ludke looked as though she wanted to foist him off on somebody else. How dare she call Will a "top scholar"? That was like calling him a geek-in-training. And how dare she stick him with this new kid? Baby-sitting this loser was the last thing Will wanted to do. The very last thing in the whole wide world.

Not only was the kid as short, fat, and bull-doggy as Mrs. Ludke herself, but he also had that awful, embarrassing, nerdy name.

The desks were set in rows of four on either side of a wide space down the middle of the classroom. Henry Higgenbotham walked, with the uncertain expression of a new dog having his tail sniffed by the rest of the pack, to the desk beside Will. His neatly creased black slacks, white button-up-the-front shirt, and—no kidding—honest-to-God bow tie seemed to emphasize the fact that he didn't belong. Everybody else wore blue jeans and sweatshirts. Cool sweatshirts, with major league logos across the chest.

Henry's light red hair was parted on one side and neatly combed. In fact the only thing out of place about Henry Higgenbotham was the slapdash streak of freckles that leaped across his nose from one cheek to the other. And maybe the round wire-frame glasses that kept sliding down his nose.

Henry smiled tentatively at Will as he sat down. He obviously wanted to be friendly.

Will didn't smile back.

"Blubberbottom gonna be your new best friend, Stinkle?" David dug a sharp elbow into Will's side. Now that he wasn't copying he had given up any pretense of being nice. Will looked straight ahead, trying to ignore the boys sitting on either side of him.

"Hey, Wee Willie Winkle! How 'bout if we just call you two Bigbottom and Dinkle? Sounds like a couple of circus clowns to me. A regular big top act. Whaddya think? Fits real good, huh,

Dink?"

Some things are hard to ignore. Will turned to his tormentor, wanting to put him roughly in his place with a biting, sarcastic remark. Unfortunately the only thing he could think to say was, "No way."

Then the bell rang, and Will scooped up his books and dived for the door. "Hey, Stinkle-Winkle. Don't forget your pet geek," yelled David after him, roaring with laughter. "Hey! Come back, Will the Finkle. Biggenbottom needs you to help him feel at home!"

But Will left the new kid to fend for himself. He had enough problems without being saddled with a scuzzbucket like Henry.

General

If Will had been paying attention to where he was going instead of thinking about getting a dog, the whole thing might never have happened.

After two years Will figured his bike could practically steer along his newspaper route by itself and never miss a porch. But he didn't figure on the two-year-old on the tricycle. The little redhead suddenly came toot-tooting her toy horn, pedaling around a car in the driveway Will was riding past.

The girl looked up at Will in surprise. Her blue eyes grew large above her freckled cheeks, but she didn't move. She just sat there, tooting her squeaky toy horn. A quick swerve off the sidewalk left the kid unharmed, but it sent Will's old blue road bike careening down the bumpy slope into Mrs. Kingston's yard. He swerved again, barely missing the white picket fence that divided her yard from her neighbor's.

It was the same route he used to take as a shortcut. But Will had promised his mother not to use it anymore after Mrs. Kingston called to complain that he was killing her grass and ruining her petunias.

Will pushed his stomach back down out of his throat with a conscious effort. Still rolling along, he grabbed a folded newspaper from the cloth carrier slung from his shoulder, balancing its weight in his right hand.

The solid thunking sound that should have accompanied his overhand throw never came. Instead the paper rattled down the width of the widow Kingston's slate shingle roof and landed with one end caught on the lip of her rain gutter.

"Rats," muttered Will, turning his front wheel for a fast stop. He miscalculated his momentum on the slick grass. The bike slid sideways, pitching Will onto the flagstone path that ran from the porch to the sidewalk. He landed on his side, with his right elbow and knee taking the hardest impact and his chin scraping painfully against the hard surface as he rolled onto his stomach.

The bike continued in the opposite direction,

slamming into the fancy latticework that covered the open space under the porch. The brittle sound of splintering wood was as loud as a gunshot in Will's ears.

Will pushed up gingerly to a sitting position just as the widow's front door flew open and she hurried out with a pink hairbrush in one hand and the collar of her big tan German shepherd grasped tightly in the other. The dog came almost to her waist. With each snarling bark he pulled his lips back to display large white teeth and slobbered long drools of spit.

Half of Mrs. Kingston's gray hair was in tight pin curls, the other half flying wildly around her pointed face. She would not have looked the least bit imposing except for the dog. The dog managed to look impressive even wearing the silly pink-flowered scarf Lydia Kingston had tied in a lopsided bow around his neck.

"Shut up, now, General," she hissed, transferring the brush into the same hand that held the dog's collar, as she reached down to button the bottom two buttons of her pink-and-orange-flowered housecoat.

"You're that William Winkle boy, aren't you? The one who ruined my petunias? What's going on out here?"

Will stood up, brushing dirt and grass from the knees of his blue jeans. One pants leg was torn, and his hand came away bloody. His elbow throbbed and his chin felt stiff with pain. He could feel a warm trickle on his neck.

"I'm sorry, Mrs. Kingston. I guess the bike slipped. It was an accident."

Now, that was a stupid thing to say, Will thought as Lydia Kingston scowled at him. Of course it was an accident. Who would mess himself up like this on purpose?

Apparently she didn't agree.

"Accident, my foot! You deliberately rode across here after your mother promised me you wouldn't. I'm going to have to call her again and give her a piece of my mind."

"No, please, it was an accident."

"Look here, you've messed up my porch and ruined my grass. I should call the paper office and have you fired." Her eyes darted from side to side in a nervous dance. She looked at Will's black tennis shoes, at his short-cropped blond hair, and over his shoulder. She only glanced briefly at his face, never meeting his eyes. "I should sic my dog on you. *He'd* teach you a thing or two. Coming along and messing up my yard and my house and then trying to tell me it's an 'accident.' Just look how you've upset General."

The dog continued to growl, a sound that rumbled menacingly through his wide, muscular chest.

"I'm really sorry about your porch, Mrs. Kingston. Really. I promise I'll pay for the damage."

"Oh, you'll pay for it, all right. But I'm still the

one who's gonna have to find somebody to do the work. I'm the one who's gonna have to hear them banging. I'm the one who's gonna have to use my back door when they have their tools all over my porch. I'm the one who's gonna have to check all the time to see they do it right. Just look at this mess. It's gonna cost me . . . I don't know . . . maybe a hundred dollars. No. That's not nearly enough. A hundred fifty dollars. Maybe even two hundred dollars. Do you have that kind of money, William Winkle?"

"Two hundred dollars?" Will swallowed hard and looked around the yard as though the answer were lodged in a bush or a tree and would pop right out at him. He had ninety-seven dollars in his savings account, and he was saving that to buy a dog. He wanted a purebred puppy with American Kennel Club papers. Not just any dog. Something special. He stopped by the animal shelter every week just to look at the dogs and dream.

"I'll give you as much as I can. For the rest, well . . . maybe you could let me make it up by working for you. I could clean out your garage. Or mow your lawn. I could mow your lawn all summer."

A large cream-colored Persian cat padded confidently past Will and up the porch steps. It rubbed one way against Mrs. Kingston's feet, then turned and rubbed the other. It was the first time Will had seen the old lady smile. General gave the cat a warning growl.

Will limped forward to retrieve his bike. General rose from his haunches and strained toward him, chopping his low growl into a bark.

"Well, I expect you'd better do that. The garage *and* the lawn. All summer. You can maybe do that instead of payin' me. Iffen you do a good enough job. And I expect you'd better get my paper now, too. I heard you throw it on my roof. I can't read a paper on the roof, and I'm not paying for it on the roof."

"Yes, ma'am."

She twisted bobby pins out of her hair and stuffed them into her housecoat pocket with one hand while she hung on to General's collar with the other. Will propped his bent bike against the side of the steps and started slowly up them. Mrs. Kingston reluctantly moved back two paces, pulling General with her.

It was hard to bend his right knee and swing up onto the porch railing so he could grab the newspaper, but Will managed it. He had to reach far to the right to grab it, stretching out his lanky five-foot-six-inch frame like a racing greyhound stretching for the finish line. He ignored the pain as the rough denim of his jeans scraped the drying blood on his knee, making it bleed all over again.

"Here's your paper, Mrs. Kingston. I'm really

sorry for hurting your porch, and I promise it won't happen again."

"Humpf! Kids today have no respect for other people's property. Now, you go ahead and git outta here, Will Winkle, before I sic General on you. Go on now. Git. And come by Saturday morning. You can start on my lawn and maybe clean out the garage."

The pug-nosed cat sat by the screen door, daintily licking its paws and waiting to be let inside. General barked twice in agreement, tossing his head so that his slavering drool made a wet spot on Mrs. Kingston's housecoat. She didn't seem to notice.

"I really am sorry, Mrs. Kingston."

The words tasted sour in Will's mouth. He pushed his bike over the flagstones, limping beside it. The front tire had gone flat, and it made a ka-thump, ka-thump sound against the hard slabs of gray rock. He wished he could just give Mrs. Kingston back the four and a half cents he got paid for delivering her paper and forget the whole thing.

He needed to keep building his savings if he was ever going to be able to afford to buy himself a dog. A really good dog. That's what he wanted. That's what he wanted more than anything else in the world. In fact there was only one dog he could think of in the whole world that he *wouldn't* want.

General barked a deep-throated warning after him as he reached the safety of the sidewalk. Will didn't turn around, but he limped a little faster.

Lydia Kingston

General didn't mind when she kicked him.

In the dark, drafty barn, where he'd lived with all the other dogs before he came here, the man who brought their food often kicked him out of the way if he crowded in too close. He was almost used to kicking.

But he did mind when the woman twisted his collar in her hand so that it dug into his neck and made it hard to swallow.

She jerked him hard as they turned to go back into the house, forcing him to scramble frantically across the brown-painted boards of the porch to keep from being strangled.

She was angry, but General couldn't understand what he'd done wrong. He'd barked at the boy . . . the boy who smelled of grass and rubber tires. He could almost taste the saltiness of the boy's other smells, the sweat and the blood, and it made his mouth sticky with thirst. Maybe he could sneak into the bathroom and drink from the big bowl when they got inside. Maybe she wouldn't smack him if he did.

She liked him to bark at strangers. That couldn't be why she was angry. Sometimes she yelled and stamped with him when he barked. He almost liked her then.

But if he got too excited and jumped on her, or leaped at the door, if he forgot himself, she always slapped him sharply across his nose, just on the spot where the old cut made his skin tender.

He'd been trying to follow the farm boy–the one who smelled like chewing tobacco and chocolate. With all those frantic puppies yapping and squealing in the rickety wooden pens all around him, he hadn't heard the man tell him to get back in the barn.

He'd only heard the boy's cheerful whistle as he headed for the open fields. He wanted to follow the boy. He wanted it so bad that he hadn't heard the heavy leather whip cracking down on his nose until it was too late.

"Git in there, you old mutt." She shoved him roughly forward through the door, but General kept his feet and tentatively wagged his tail. The one thing he never smelled on her was fear. The boy had given off the tang of fear when General barked at him. It was a musky, foul-smelling odor that humans never seemed to recognize. General hated that smell.

He would have liked to stay outside and run, but she never let him. He whined softly.

"Aw, shut up." She slapped his rump, but he didn't feel it. General tried to push away the memory of the farm and the time the farm boy had taken him out in the corn fields to run joyously up and down the furrows. Sometimes he felt such a longing–to run and run, to roll in the dirt, and chase the droning bees he heard buzzing outside the windows. He whined again, but this time she ignored him and padded out to the kitchen in her fuzzy pink slippers.

General trotted to the bathroom and nudged open the door. As he plunged his muzzle into the bowl he thought again about the smells of the boy, smells that mixed with his longings like gravy mixed with the dry pieces of his food . . . into one delicious daydream.

By Any Other Name

"Did you get Mrs. Kingston?" It was the first thing his mother asked when he walked into the green-tiled kitchen with its friendly smells of peeled oranges and baking chicken.

"Yup."

"Did you know she called the newspaper office yesterday to complain that you missed her? And she called last week to complain that you didn't bag her paper when it looked like rain," his mother continued, handing him a black plastic garbage bag from under the sink. His mother was so busy doing two things at once that she didn't really look at him. "Lydia Kingston's one customer you have to pay special attention to, Will. She's quick to complain. Ever since Alfred Kingston died last year, she's been short-tempered with everyone. But we shouldn't blame her. She's obviously nervous about living alone. So you have to be especially considerate around her, Will. And *not* make excuses. Now, take this and start with the trash in the kitchen. You missed *it* yesterday, too."

Will grabbed the bag and shook it open with a whoosh. "I *didn't* miss her yesterday. Her dog probably ate it and she just decided to blame it on me." He knew he was making an excuse, but he couldn't stop himself.

"Well, I *know* you missed the trash. So get on it. You still have time before dinner. Bryan!" She called out to his younger brother in the living room. "I want you to set the table."

"I have to go to the bathroom," came the instant response.

"Well, hurry up," their mom called back. Then she turned to Will with a knowing smile. "How come you two always have to go to the bathroom when there's a chore to be done? Good grief, Will, what happened to you? You're bleeding! Are you okay? You didn't break any bones, did you?" His mother sounded worried as she surveyed his ripped blue jeans and scraped skin.

"It's nothing. I hit a pothole and the bike threw me. No big deal. As soon as bratface gets out of the bathroom, I'll go wash up."

His mother looked doubtful, but she returned

to her sink full of fresh-scrubbed vegetables. "Be sure to get all the dirt out. And spray some anti-septic on the scrapes," she cautioned. "I some-times think the paper ought to give you danger pay for doing that route."

"I wish." Will nodded his agreement and shoved a jumble of empty cereal boxes, banana peels, and crumpled aluminum foil from the kitchen trash into a more compact lump at the bottom of the garbage bag. "By the way, Mom, Mrs. Kingston wants me to come over Saturday to help her with some yard work."

"You didn't have another run-in with her, did you, Will?" It was hard to believe, but his mom's uncanny mother radar had already picked up the fact that he wasn't telling her the whole story. "Not when you know how picky she is. She keeps her house and yard cleaner than a cat keeps its fur. You didn't mess up her yard, did you?"

"It wasn't my fault," Will protested, focusing his gaze on the garbage as he confessed every-thing. "Mrs. Kingston's yard is full of potholes and my bike bounced in one and then slid into her porch. That's not my fault, is it? But she yelled at me anyway. And her dog almost bit me. And now I gotta go over Saturday and do yard work for her. And my bike has a flat tire. But you don't see *me* making her come change it. It's not fair." Will gave the garbage bag a vicious kick, then swung it up over his shoulder. "It's not fair," he repeated.

Before his mother could answer, Bryan appeared at the kitchen door in a Dogs Are Man's Best Friend T-shirt Will had outgrown. "It's Will's turn to set the table," he whined. "I did it yesterday."

"Will's doing the garbage," their mom said shortly, busily chopping celery into a big bowl of cut-up apples.

"How come I have to do all the work?" It was Bryan's continual complaint.

"You don't do *any* work, snorthead. When you're only nine you don't even know what work is." Will shouldered past him, purposely knocking into him with the half-stuffed garbage bag.

Bryan shoved back, knocking Will into the door frame. "Oh yeah? Like a twelve-year-old apeface would really know. Blow it out your kazoo, dorkbreath!"

Will pinched Bryan's arm sharply and hurried off into the dining room.

"Mom!" Bryan exploded. "Will pinched me!" Bryan followed him into the dining room carrying a fistful of spoons, knives, and forks he'd just scooped out of the silverware drawer. He pointedly jabbed a fork into Will's rear end.

Will dropped the garbage bag and lunged for Bryan's neck, grabbing him easily in a loose headlock.

"Mom!" screamed Bryan.

"Boys!" came their mother's warning voice. "Do you want to spend the next hour alone in your rooms? I'll separate you if I have to. . . ." She let the sentence trail off, but her sharp tone made it clear that she meant business.

"We're just fooling around, Mom," Will called back in a reassuring voice.

"Don't be such a baby," he whispered in Bryan's ear, momentarily tightening and then dropping the headlock. "Or I'll sic Mrs. Kingston's killer dog on you."

"You mean old Buzzard Breath?"

"I mean General, Mrs. Kingston's big ugly German shepherd attack dog. You know. Old lady Kingston. Five sixty-seven North Maple Street."

"Yeah, I know," Bryan agreed, dumping the silverware on the table and plucking napkins from the napkin basket on the big maple sideboard. "Buzzard Breath."

"Since when?" Will had grabbed the living room trash can just around the edge of the arched opening between the living room and the dining room and was vigorously shaking it into his bag.

"Since David White heard him snoring. I heard Dave talking about it on the bus last week. Dave says Mrs. Kingston's dog snores like a buzz saw and he oughta be called Buzzard

Breath. Dave says he snuck up close and the dumb mutt didn't even hear him, he was making so much noise. Dave says his breath smells like dead fish, too. You know. Like something a big old buzzard would eat. So that makes him Buzzard Breath. Pretty neat, huh? I can't figure how that guy comes up with this stuff."

"Dave's a genius," said Will flatly.

"Have you finished the garbage yet, Willie?" called their mother. "I need you to pour drinks for dinner."

"Almost." Will turned to his brother with a questioning look. "Dave says, Dave says–why do people listen to that creep?"

"He's funny when he makes fun of teachers and stuff. You should have heard him talking about some new kid named Henry. He was a riot. Besides, he's practically an adult. He's sixteen or something."

"Yeah. An adult still in the sixth grade," Will said sarcastically. "And for your information, he's only fourteen. Besides, why's he picking on Mrs. Kingston's dog? I wonder . . ."

"Wonder what?" asked Bryan, shoving the final napkin under the last spoon and knife.

"Will! Hurry up!"

"Coming," called Will, winking at Bryan. "Forget it. Next time General acts like he wants to take a bite outta me, I think I'll call his bluff."

"Here's your father's car," their mom called as

both boys recognized the familiar sound of their dad's silver-gray Volkswagen van pulling up the driveway to stop outside the kitchen door.

"Coming," yelled Will again. He laughed softly as he flipped the black plastic garbage bag closed with a twist of his wrist. "You won't scare me again, General. Or 'Buzzard Breath.' Or whatever your name is. Come Saturday we'll just see how fierce you are."

Saturday in the Salt Mines

The first thing wrong with Saturday morning was that he had to get up so early. His mom actually called him at 9 a.m. Usually on Saturdays he hung in bed till almost noon and then slugged around the house for an hour or so until it was time for a pickup game of football or baseball or a run to the mall. But this morning he was due at Lydia Kingston's house.

The second thing wrong with Saturday morning was that he had to see Mrs. Kingston and her dog again–and this time it would be up close and personal. Will had felt better about it after his talk with Bryan last night, but now, in the warm May sunshine, he wasn't so sure General wasn't still a General–tough, mean, and in charge–instead of a silly old Buzzard Breath.

Will gulped down the glass of orange juice his mom put at his place at the table, stuffed a piece of toast into his mouth, and jammed a banana into his jeans pocket. He chewed quickly, swallowed noisily, and yelled, "Later, Mom," as he slammed the screen door in the kitchen on his way out to his bike. He was glad he'd taken the time to fix the tire last night.

His mom yelled something back, something like "be careful" or "watch the traffic" or one of those things she always said when he was on his way out. She had about a dozen of them. Will figured she could just number them one to twelve and then yell "three" or maybe "nine" as he left the house and he'd know just what she meant.

He arrived at Lydia Kingston's slightly run-down white-shingle house within five minutes. The broken latticework under the porch looked like the opening to some trollish cave, and Will half expected the big tan dog to emerge from the black hole and grab him.

Instead, after he leaned his bike up against the corner rainspout, he heard the click-click-click of hedge clippers and the high-pitched warble of Mrs. Kingston's scratchy voice singing "row, row, row your boat."

He certainly hoped she wouldn't ask him to

sing rounds with her. He'd rather give her every penny in his savings account–and maybe his firstborn someday.

"Mrs. Kingston?" he called, walking around some rhododendron bushes at the side of the house.

"Is that you, William Winkle? I certainly hope so. It's about time you got here, young man. I locked General up in the spare room, so he won't be bothering us. There's lots to do. Lots and lots to do."

She started Will on the lawn mower. It was a power mower, but an old one, and it seemed to sputter and choke to a stop anywhere the grass was thick or anytime he tried to pull it backward. It made the job of mowing the lawn twice as hard as it should have been.

After the lawn Will raked grass clippings, and after that she made him saw a dead branch off the dogwood tree by the shed.

Will was red-faced and thirsty by the time Mrs. Kingston finally suggested they stop for a drink. He figured the slight bulge on her stooped old back was probably like a camel's hump. She could probably store water and live in the desert with no problem. She definitely has a face like a camel, thought Will. Or maybe it's more like the face of an Irish wolfhound–kind of square and whiskery.

"Go in the kitchen and get yourself a cup of

lemonade from the refrigerator," she said with her wide camel lips. "And bring me one, too."

Will turned gratefully and bounded up her creaky back steps. "Right," he called over his shoulder. "Comin' up!" He slammed into the room and was past the red Formica kitchen table and halfway to the squat white refrigerator in the corner when he was suddenly struck by the third thing wrong with this Saturday morning. The third thing was the movement he saw out of the corner of his eye. The movement was General.

Will looked around frantically for a weapon. A stick. A knife. A bazooka.

The tan shepherd with the black-tipped ears and tail advanced slowly and silently, backing him into a corner of the kitchen. The only thing within reach was a chrome-and-vinyl chair. Will grabbed it and brandished it in front of him, lion tamer-style.

The dog cocked his head to one side and lowered his rear haunches silently to the floor. He wasn't making that low, rumbling growl he'd made yesterday. His soft brown eyes were locked on Will's.

"She *said* you were shut up in the bedroom. So how come you're in the kitchen?" Will's voice sounded loud in the stillness of the room. The only other noises were the hum of the refrigerator and the ticking of the yellow kitchen clock on the wall.

The dog simply sat and watched him.

"She wants some lemonade. From the fridge." Will lowered the chair and leaned against the back of it as he explained. "You know, I don't think I've ever seen a solid-color German shepherd before. You're not too bad. You're practically good looking."

The sound of the ticking clock was joined by the slow thump-thump of General's tail hitting the yellow-and-brown linoleum floor. Will moved cautiously around the chair and slid down into it. The vinyl cushion wheezed. Slowly Will stuck out his right hand, palm down.

"How about if I touch you? Would you hurt me? Or could we maybe be friends?"

The dog stood up in one smooth movement and advanced toward Will's hand. He was growling now, so softly that it sounded like a purr. The feathery end of his tail flicked back and forth. His nose felt cold as it touched Will's fingers.

"Hey, would you like a glass of lemonade, too?" Will was almost whispering. The black nose seemed to hover, undecided, over the bandage on Will's index finger. He'd skinned it when he took that header off his bike.

"Or maybe a soda–or ice water–or jeez, a beer, I don't know. Anything you want. Whaddaya say? You thirsty, too?"

The dog's tongue felt rough and wet against Will's hand. Will dropped off the chair onto his knees and reached forward, running his hand gently up over the scar on the dark velvety muzzle and stopping to scratch between the ears.

"You're a great big fake, aren't ya? All bark. No bite." Will ran both hands down the dog's flanks and under his belly as Buzzard Breath sat perfectly still.

Because he *was* Buzzard Breath. He had a friendly, almost clownish expression that wasn't the least bit military. This canine was no fierce General of a guard dog.

Will put his face close to Buzz's and touched the tip of his snout with the tip of his own nose. Buzz's breath was warm and doggy, but nothing to make you puke, thought Will, scratching under the shepherd's chin. Nothing fierce or scary here. This dog was a regular pussycat.

Bathsheba, Mrs. Kingston's long-haired Persian cat, flashed silently past them, making Will jump. Buzzard Breath ignored the cat's quick swipe at his tail and pressed closer to Will. The cat disappeared around the kitchen counter.

"Where's my lemonade, William Winkle?" Mrs. Kingston's faraway voice floated through the screen door.

Will stood up and hurried over to the refrigerator. Bathsheba glared at him from her perch between a mug tree and a fancy wine bottle atop the freezer. Buzz followed Will closely, long nails clicking on the faded linoleum.

Will grabbed the frosted pitcher of lemonade, making the ice rattle. He spotted a plastic baggie wrapped around a single hot dog and grabbed that, too, shaking the wiener onto the floor for Buzz.

Then he took a long drink straight from the pitcher. When he ran out of breath he set the pitcher on the floor and let Buzz slurp lemonade from it as he got a glass from the cabinet above the sink. He snatched the pitcher away from Buzz, poured out a glass, and took another few gulps for himself. There was barely enough lemonade left to cover the bottom of the pitcher. But Will replaced it on the wire shelf anyway.

Bathsheba hissed as he slammed the refrigerator door and yelled, "Coming, Mrs. Kingston. Be there in a minute."

"You better get back in the spare room," he whispered to Buzz, leading the dog into the room across the hall. He bent down and gave the shepherd a quick hug, then pushed him in and banged the door shut firmly. "If she wants to know tonight who drank all the lemonade, you can blame it on me, okay?" he called through the door.

Buzz barked three times. Will felt as if the dog could sense his hand laid against the smooth wood between them. He grinned, suddenly feeling that this was a pretty darn good

Saturday, even though he still had to help Mrs. Kingston. "See ya, Buzz," he called, and the dog barked again, almost as if he recognized the name.

Henry

It was what his dad jokingly called the "new American good-bye." People said "see ya" or "talk to ya later." Nobody ever said good-bye. Good-bye was too final.

When he'd left Mrs. Kingston's after finishing her chores, he'd said "see ya" to General. He hadn't thought it might be the last time he'd ever see the dog.

Not that he cared. He just couldn't seem to stop thinking about it.

Mrs. Kingston was out on her porch when he was finishing up the newspaper route on Monday. She was sitting on the green metal glider, rocking back and forth with Bathsheba stretched out and purring on her lap. There was no sign of Buzz. So Will asked about him.

That got her started. Mrs. Kingston went on and on, as if she'd just been waiting for somebody to ask about General so she could tell all about what a rotten guard dog he'd been. It sounded as though she were trying to convince herself.

"I swear, that dog mighta looked tough, like a big ol' sour ball. But he was sugar on a stick when it came to kids. These neighborhood kids could tease him, tramp through my yard, ruin my petunias and my tulips, even pull the dog's tail, and he wouldn't do nothin' more than bark a little. I don't think he'd ever bite anybody. Even if they was killing me."

Smart dog, thought Will, but out loud he said, "So where is he? What did ya do with him?"

"I called my brother-in-law, Howard. The one what trained him. I told Howard to take him back and bring me a real guard dog. He's comin' out tonight."

"Then where's General?" Will hoped he could at least go into the house and say good-bye.

"He run off. Funny, is'n'it? You go fixing to get rid of a dog and it's like he knows, and he just ups and leaves on his own. But Howard'll find him when he comes out tonight. And he'll take him on back to the farm."

That seemed to be that.

Will had propped his bike against the bottom step as he handed Lydia Kingston her afternoon paper, and now he remounted and rode quickly down her sidewalk to her driveway and the street.

Her house was right behind Will's, sort of. It was on the other side of the tree-covered hill that served as the town's watershed. Cutting through the woods took just a few minutes. Going around the hill on the road, however, took a hard five minutes of uphill pedaling.

Will's throat was feeling all sticky and tight, as if he'd swallowed something too big and it hadn't gone down right.

But that was dumb. He'd only known General a little while, after all. And the shepherd had never been the right dog for him. He wasn't saving up for an ordinary old German shepherd. That wasn't what he wanted. Besides, the guys in the neighborhood made fun of General, calling him Buzzard Breath and laughing at the way he looked in that silly pink scarf Mrs. Kingston liked to tie around his neck.

Of course, Dave White made fun of Will's name, too, calling him "Stinkle." Dave twisted Henry Higgenbotham's name into "Blubberbottom."

The barking noise in Will's backyard surprised him as he turned up his driveway. There was Blubberbottom–Henry–with a little black dog on a leash. The animal wriggled and jumped enthusiastically, barking and yapping as Will approached them.

"Hey, Will!" Henry looked relaxed and almost normal out of the classroom. But then the whole world looked better when David White wasn't breathing down your neck.

"Thought you might like to see my dog. Since you like dogs so much."

Will parked his bike in the carport and came over to grin down at the puppy-sized canine, who stopped barking to concentrate on sniffing his tennis shoes.

"That's a nice miniature dachshund." Will offered Henry the compliment freely. True, Henry might interpret that to mean he was willing to be friends. But . . . well, heck, maybe he was. Henry had offered him a SweeTart to suck in math class that morning while Dave White had been at the principal's office. Will had even asked Henry a whispered question about common denominators.

"How do you know what kind of dog Max is?" Henry looked impressed, and Will reached down to scratch between the dog's floppy ears and rub his low-slung tummy.

"I know stuff about dogs," Will responded.

"Like I know stuff about stamps," interjected Henry, eager to join in.

It was true. Will had noticed that everybody seemed to know about something. His dad knew cars–their years, their models, even their engines. His mom knew movie stars–who starred in what, with whom, and when. His brother knew baseball–the teams, the batting averages, the players. He guessed Henry must know something about stamps, if he said he did. And Will knew dogs.

He knew, for instance, that a shar-pei had wrinkly skin, was prone to mange, and cost a whopping two thousand dollars. He knew that dachshunds were bred in Germany to chase badgers and that the little dogs were likely to have back problems as they got older. He knew so much about dogs, in fact, that he could practically write a book on the subject.

The only thing he *didn't* know was where General–where Buzzard Breath–was right now. It was funny, but that derogatory name didn't really bother him anymore. In fact he sort of liked the name Buzz.

"Max is a good name for a dachshund," Will offered, standing up and clapping a hand on Henry's shoulder. All the name-calling Henry had endured in school last week seemed long ago. Longer ago than last semester's history test.

"I have some dog stamps from the nineteen sixties." Henry jumped into the conversation eagerly. "I collect stamps. I already told you. I've got a poodle and a greyhound from Togo. That's an island in the Pacific. And I have a real neat German shepherd from Suriname." Will looked at him blankly. "That's a country in South

America. And it's a great stamp. Really rare. Well, sort of rare, anyway. A rare German shepherd," he repeated proudly. "Do you wanna come over and see it sometime?"

Will grinned at him. "Sure. I have a good friend who's a German shepherd."

Henry is okay, Will thought. And so was his name, even if it did sound a little funny. After all, what did his dad always say? The name doesn't make the person. The person makes the name.

If General were his dog, Will decided suddenly, he'd call him Buzzard Breath. The screen door banged behind them as they entered the house, and the fan whirred on the kitchen ceiling. "Want a soda?" asked Will.

"Can we give Max some water, too?" Henry pushed his glasses back up. They kept sliding down his sweaty nose.

"Sure. I already have a dog dish," Will said proudly, reaching under the sink where he stored his someday-I'm-going-to-have-a-dog gear.

Maybe, he thought, he should put some water outside for Buzz. Just in case. In case the big shepherd was back in the woods behind their house and feeling thirsty. In case Mrs. Kingston's brother-in-law couldn't find Buzz and truck him away. In case there was another chance to say good-bye.

Roadkill

The tan shepherd stood in the middle of the road, a gray squirrel dangling limply from his jaws. He was looking up the hill, waiting for the Beast to return and claim its kill.

He had watched the Beast for two days. It seemed to kill without eating, while his own hunger had driven him to eat the fat wriggling worms that appeared by the dozen after last night's rain.

The only sound was the rat-a-tat drilling of a woodpecker in the thickly wooded ravine where the dog had been hiding. He turned and trotted back toward the tangled thicket of roadside honeysuckle, with a cavelike opening tucked beneath its trailing branches.

He didn't run.

Even if the Beast suddenly roared down on top of him, it would not catch him slinking fearfully away like some mangy raccoon.

The shepherd entered its makeshift den and began to tear at the musty fur of the squirrel, sneezing as long hairs from the bushy tail tickled his nose. The smell of the warm flesh made his mouth water.

The dry nuggets of food the woman put in a dish on her kitchen floor had never smelled like this. They had crunched pleasantly between his teeth and tasted faintly of old cooked meat, but they had never smelled as good as the things the woman made for herself on the counter just above his head.

But this smelled even better. If he could just bite through these mouthfuls of choking fur . . .

A sound made him freeze, the bloody squirrel carcass balanced on his paws, his mouth half open. It was still far away–but it was the Beast's roar. It was coming from the top of the hill. It was coming back.

The shepherd clamped its jaws around the torn body of the squirrel. If he had to fight for his meal, he would fight.

He emerged from the honeysuckle thicket and stood staring at the road, almost invisible in the dark shadows of the trees. He could see it now. It wasn't the same Beast that killed the squirrel. But it was heading right at him.

Maybe it was a member of the same pack. He had seen them travel in packs before.

It was huge, a gray monster with a roar that seemed to rise and fall in grinding anger, and empty eyes that gleamed with the reflected light of the setting sun. It smelled overpoweringly of rubber and oil, an evil, unnatural odor that, he remembered, sometimes mixed with the powerful scent of humans. The Beasts and the humans were friends.

It was almost on top of him now.

The tan shepherd tensed, dropping the squirrel at his feet, ready to leap to the attack. He'd have to jump high. When he'd watched the Beast kill before, he saw that it never grabbed with its teeth or clutched with its claws. It simply used its massive bulk to run down anything in its path. He'd watched those heavy feet crush a screaming cat and smash into a fleeing groundhog that tried–too late–to turn tail and run.

Most Beasts stayed on the road, but the shepherd knew it could mow down trees and sign posts and even human fences. He'd already seen one leave the road to die, turning belly up with a great scream of protest and a gushing cloud of sooty smoke as it gasped its last breath.

When this Beast came for the squirrel, he would leap for its eyes, away from the danger of those deadly feet. He would surprise it with his speed and strength and let it blindly bash itself against the towering oaks and maples all around them.

As the Beast roared toward him on the curve–it turned. It was as though it had never seen him, even though its bright yellow eyes stared straight at him. It simply roared around the curve and disappeared into the deepening twilight, its distant guttural purr fading into a silence punctuated by the woodpecker's industrious drilling.

The dog whined. He didn't understand these Beasts any more than he understood humans. The only human who even began to make sense was the boy, the one who came into the kitchen and rubbed between his ears and gave him a cold drink. He whined again, wishing the boy were here now, with his warm salty smell and his friendly fingers that tasted like freshly mowed grass.

A waft of squirrel smell suddenly filled his nostrils, and the shepherd forgot all about everything except the sharp twist of his hungry belly. He crouched down right where he was and tore into the carcass, gulping down the chunks of meat whole.

After half a dozen bites, there was nothing left. The dog nosed the skeleton, chewing on a small bone and wishing he had a piece of meat like the one the boy had given him that day in the kitchen. A long cold tube of pungent pink meat. It was a warm night, and he didn't bother returning to his thicket den but lay beside the road, watching the moon rays trickle down the hill in a silvery spiderweb of light.

He was soon asleep, his legs drawn up under him, his head hanging over the lip of the gravel ditch beside the road. His ears twitched and the tip of his tail jerked back and forth convulsively.

He was dreaming. The boy was running down the road, calling to him, calling a name he couldn't quite hear. There was another noise filling his ears and, as he ran toward the boy, up and up the steep hill that seemed to never end, he saw the Beast, looming behind the boy, bearing down on him. He barked a warning, but the smiling boy did not seem to hear him. The dog ran faster.

But the Beast was right behind the heedless boy, ready to smash him, roaring closer and closer. . . .

The shepherd's head shot up, and he growled, deep in his throat, as he looked around at the shrouding mist floating down the road in the watery light. It was morning. A Beast suddenly roared by him, its voice immediately muffled again as it disappeared into the fog. The only sounds now were a robin's warbling, tuneless song and the early-morning chatter of a magpie.

The dog rose and stretched, turning his head to bite an itchy place near his tail. The stolen squirrel was a distant memory as hunger grabbed his insides and clawed at them. There was another smell in the air, a familiar, deliciously sizzling smell, like the meat the woman used to fry in the big black skillet. Twice she had let him lick the grease. Even though he burned his tongue a little the first time, it had been wonderful.

Without even thinking where he was going, the dog turned downhill, toward his former home. He trotted through the woods with a sure sense of direction, pausing once to lap up a puddle of morning dew that glistened in the deep depression of a mossy rock.

The bacon smell that had tickled his nose back at the road had disappeared. Now there was another smell–the distinctive, separate odors of other dogs. Two. No, three of them. All together. Loping through these same woods toward the road he had just left. Now he could hear the twigs snapping and the leaves rustling under their running feet. A warning growl rumbled deep in his chest, but they passed him, just out of sight, without even slowing down.

The shepherd waited, to be sure they were gone, and resumed his course toward home. It wasn't really home anymore, of course. He'd run away when the woman kicked him. It wasn't the kick so much as the wide-open door behind her. He had barreled past her and out that door as though something outside were calling to him. He hadn't run far. He'd simply hung around at the edge of the woods behind the house. He'd seen the boy come by. He'd almost come out then. But something had held him back.

He'd come halfway down the hill when he saw the man. The woman had given his leash to the same big, sour-smelling man who had brought him here, riding in the wagon behind one of those squat, round-nosed, wagon-pulling Beasts.

The man had spotted him and shouted angrily at him, his heavy feet thudding up the hill toward the dog.

"You come down here and git in the back of this here truck, you dad-blamed stupid dog!"

The man had yelled some more and whistled a few times. He had snapped his fingers and waved his arms over his head. But with only two feet to run on, the man lumbered like a turtle. Soon his angry shouts were only echoes in the quiet places of the great woods. The man couldn't catch him.

Now the dog stopped as he came to the brown-shingled house, with its wide, sagging porch and odors of dusty wood and human sweat. Yes! Yes. There was the same sweet odor of frying meat he remembered . . . and there was a new smell.

The hackles on his neck rose. His tail froze in midair, and a snarl curled his black lips.

A sudden explosion of barking split the quiet morning. The sound came from inside the house. It was followed by the woman's impatient scolding. "Shush now, Assassin! You stop! I won't have you goin' crazy over ev'ry creature that skitters by out there. Good Lord, ya almost make me wish I had General back agin. Now here, you can have these bacon leavings, if you stop your growling, and I'll just look out this window and find out what's got your withers all ablaze."

Her pale, squinting face, with a crown of pin curls, appeared at the kitchen door, looking out into the empty backyard. The tan shepherd disappeared.

Designated Hero

What did ya do to my bike?"

"Nothin'."

"Look at the fender. It's bent and the paint's scratched. And the tire's flat. After I just fixed it up. What did you do to it?"

"Nothin'," repeated Bryan with a stubborn jut of his chin.

"Well, it sure wasn't like this yesterday. I know you rode it to do the papers while I was helping Mrs. Kingston pick up the new lattice for her porch. What happened?"

"Your dumb bike broke. That's what happened. I think you musta fixed it wrong, 'cause it didn't steer right and it ran me right into a tree. It coulda killed me."

"A bike is an inanimate object," stated Will, quoting his father. "It only does what *you* make it do."

"I should probably sue you for . . . well . . . you know . . . maybe wrongful bike fixing or . . . I should send you a writ of habeas corpus for pain and suffering and stuff like that, but I figured, since you're my brother, I'd overlook it this time." Bryan definitely watched too many lawyer shows on television. In fact, the kid had recently decided he was going to *be* a lawyer when he grew up. Last month, after a class trip to a bakery, he'd wanted to be a pastry chef. Last year, after dressing up as Batman at Halloween, he was sure he'd grow up to be a superhero.

Will shook his head in disgust. Kids!

"*You* broke it. It didn't break itself." Will shoved his wallet back into his jeans pocket. "And I don't see why I should have to pay you for subbing when you ruined my bike."

"You better pay me." Bryan danced back out of reach, sticking out his tongue. "Mom won't like it if I tell her you won't pay me."

"I'll tell her about the bike."

"She'll say you shouldn'ta let me take your bike if it wasn't fixed right, 'cause I coulda gotten hurt. Maybe you'd better pay me double."

"In your dreams, weaselface." Reluctantly Will pulled his wallet out again and counted out three wrinkled dollar bills, flinging them angrily at

Bryan. "Now I have to walk and it's gonna take me twice as long as usual. And you know Dad was going to drive me to the shelter tonight." He looked at his brother pleadingly. "You could help me deliver. That would be fair."

"Sure," Bryan agreed lazily. "For three more dollars."

"You little ferret. You're not getting any more money out of me after what you did to my bike. It'll cost me ten dollars to take it into the shop."

"Have it your way. Anyway, I don't want to run into that dog pack again. They're mean suckers. Remember what I told you last night? Dad thinks they're just strays, but I didn't tell him how they chased me. And I think old Buzzard Breath is the leader. He's the meanest one."

"He's okay. He wouldn't hurt anybody."

"I don't know about that. Since Mrs. Kingston chucked him out, I think he's gone bad. You should get yourself a new route. The old one's gettin' too dangerous. Besides, I don't have time for newspapers. I got to level six on Double Dragon yesterday. Today I'm gonna try and beat it."

"I'll give you a buck," Will offered grudgingly.

"No way." Bryan waved the three dollars in a triumphant salute. "The video game master must play. Later, dude."

Will charged him, skirting around the pile of unfolded papers in front of him, but sliding clumsily on a layer of orange plastic bags scattered beside them. Bryan dodged cheerfully into the house, still waving the dollar bills like a victory banner over his head.

Will dusted off his bottom, where several of the newspaper bags were hanging, attached by the static of his slide. Dumb kid! Bryan didn't care about getting a dog. The only animal that could hold Bryan's attention was the sonic hedgehog in his video games.

But Will had to get moving if he was going to make that trip to the kennel with his dad tonight. His father had warned him that it might take a long time to find "the perfect dog." But since both of them enjoyed looking at dogs, they visited the shelter pretty much every week. They went to dog shows, too, and they stopped at the pet store every time his mom shopped at the mall. It had been three months since Will's twelfth birthday, when his parents had finally declared him to be old enough to "buy and take care of" his very own dog. That's when the search had started.

His dad definitely favored the shelter dogs. That's why they went so often. He said, when you got a dog as a puppy, you were stuck. It might be a whiner. It might be a barker. It might be a jumper. A puppy was like a baby. You took what you got and you learned to live with it.

Older dogs, on the other hand, already had set

personalities. And at the shelter you could get to know a dog gradually–sort of like making a friend. Or, as his dad put it, a little like getting married. When it was right you'd know it. Bells would ring.

Will didn't think the shelter was the place where he'd discover his dream dog, but he desperately wanted to hear those bells. And it never hurt to look.

In the meantime Will hummed the tune of "Tonight, Tonight," from his mom's tape of *West Side Story*. She was always listening to movie sound tracks and Broadway musicals, and sometimes the songs just sort of stuck in his head. Last night she'd been watching some TV movie and complaining that there was no suspense because she already knew the hero was going to live. She'd explained to Will that when a guy was "the designated hero," he always survived.

Will switched from humming to whistling tunelessly as he rolled and rubber-banded each paper. He jammed each rolled paper into a slick fluorescent orange bag, twisting each bag neatly closed with the speed of long practice.

That was what he wanted to be when he grew up. A designated hero. That would be great. To know that things were always going to turn out okay, no matter what. He bet the Punisher didn't waste his time worrying about people who called him names. And Terminator probably never had to put up with a nerdy, smart-mouthed little brother either.

But in real life the chances of being a hero seemed pretty small. Will figured he was more likely to *need* saving than to *do* the saving.

If only life were more like the movies, he'd get his dog. Buzzard Breath would get a great new home. And Bryan would discover that Mom and Dad weren't his real parents and go live someplace else.

Trouble

It was the same dog he'd been seeing for the past month, maybe the one Bryan had seen yesterday–the tan, beagle-looking hound with the torn ear and the dirty coat. It skulked along the edge of the woods, disappearing into the shadows and then suddenly appearing again, carefully paralleling Will's own steps.

Will looked around for a stick or a rock. This mutt had sometimes nipped at his heels when he was on his bike. Today with the bike out of commission, it would be impossible to outrun the little mongrel.

Will had already been bitten once, about a year ago, when he tried to deliver a paper to the back porch of a lady who usually kept her dog inside. He hadn't been worried when the dog approached him, had, in fact, even started to pet the mutt when it opened its mouth and bit him. Right on the calf. Didn't break the skin, but it left a ring of tooth-shaped bruises that hurt for the rest of the day.

Ever since that happened, Will had been reluctant to let any strange dog get too close. He stopped and twisted a branch off a nearby pine tree, ignoring the sticky needles. He had to tug it loose from the trunk after cracking it off, but it made a satisfying whistling noise when he whipped it through the air to test its heft.

"You stay away." He spoke directly to the watching dog, brandishing his new weapon. "Don't bother me, and I won't bother you."

Will shivered and buttoned the top button of his navy blue jacket as he noticed a second dog, smaller than the first, following along with the hound, a few yards farther back in the woods. This one was some kind of an ugly terrier mix, a squat, snub-nosed dog with wiry rust-colored hair that stood in messy spikes across the top of his head and hung halfway across its eyes. Like the first dog, it didn't bark or growl or wave its tail. It just watched him, moving when he moved, stopping when he stopped, and always maintaining its distance.

Will quickened his pace. He hadn't believed Bryan when he'd said he was chased by a pack of wild dogs on the route yesterday. Bryan was always making things up, just to bug him. The kid watched too many Saturday morning cartoons. That was all.

But what if Bryan hadn't been lying?

Will grabbed the strap of his newspaper bag to keep it from sliding off his shoulder as he started to jog up Ridge Avenue. This part of the route went through the woods, and there were only a couple of newly built houses up on the left-hand side. He wasn't even sure if anybody lived in those houses yet. One had a Sold sign in the straw-covered-mud front yard but no curtains in the empty black windows. The other one still had a For Sale sign leaning against the whitewashed mailbox post.

Will felt, rather than heard, the third dog. It was a sudden realization that made the hairs on the nape of his neck tingle. Something was moving behind him. He was sure of it.

He wanted to drop the bag of newspapers and run. He wanted to yell for help at the top of his lungs. But most of all he wanted to turn around and discover that it was all his imagination. That nothing was behind him and that every dog in the woods had scurried off to chase squirrels.

Will's steps slowed. He glanced over at the edge of the trees, three yards to his left. There was no sign of his shadowy pursuers.

He came to a complete stop and slowly

turned, a grin turning up his pursed lips. He felt silly. Good thing Bryan couldn't see him now. The kid would die laughing.

Will's grin vanished with a gasp. They were there. It hadn't been his imagination. The beagle-sized hound, the runty terrier, and a third dog all stood looking at him. The third dog was a big hound, or maybe a Labrador mix. He was black with short floppy ears and a long bushy tail, but his shaggy coat was ragged and matted with mud. He was the thinnest of the lot, but they all looked hungry and restless.

The big dog, the obvious leader, began to growl, a chilling sound, deep in his throat. His lip curled in a sort of canine sneer, revealing large yellow teeth.

Where had they come from? Will fought down the urge to run wildly up the hill. Who did they belong to? And, most importantly, what was he supposed to do now?

The one thing he was sure of was that it would be a mistake to turn his back on this lot. He began to speak, in what he hoped was a soft steady voice. "Come on now, guys. I don't have anything you want. I'm not bothering you. I'm just passing through."

Slowly, step by step, he backed away from the dogs as he spoke. "Go on, now. Go home. Get outta here, you ugly mutts. Leave me alone. I've got all these papers to deliver. I don't have time for this. Go chase some rabbits and just *leave me alone!*" He raised his voice with those last words.

The big black hound took a step forward. That was, apparently, too much for the tightly wound terrier, who came suddenly charging at Will, yapping excitedly. Will swatted the creature's snout with the pine branch as it neared him. Yelping as though it had just been severely beaten, the cowardly little runt scurried back behind his leader.

"Get outta here!" Will shouted, waving the branch in as threatening a manner as he could. The black hound ignored him and began to advance, its muffled growl now a full-throated snarl.

Will brandished the pine limb in front of him like a sword. The other two dogs were right behind their leader, showing their own teeth in almost comic mimicry of the big black hound. Will looked around desperately for a better weapon or a route of escape.

What he saw made him drop the branch. The sack of papers slid unnoticed off his shoulder. It was Buzzard Breath. Mrs. Kingston's killer German shepherd was running toward the rest of the pack, flat out, through the woods. Its light tan coat flashed in and out of the shadows, like a ray of bright sunshine dancing through the dark greens and deep browns of the forest. An incongruous pink scarf waved like a tattered battle flag around his neck.

Will turned and began to sprint wildly up the hill. If Buzzard Breath was the leader of this scraggly neighborhood dog pack, he was dead meat.

The impatient terrier had surged ahead again. Its jaws closed over the heel of Will's sneaker.

Will turned and tried to shake it off. He lifted his foot and swung it in a wide arc, unexpectedly catching the black hound across the side of the head.

Both dog and shoe were knocked loose. Will lost his balance, sprawling backward onto the gravel that formed a narrow shoulder beside the black macadam of the road.

The tan shepherd was practically on top of them now. Will's hands flew up to his neck. He could almost feel the slavering jaws closing over his jugular vein. He wondered for a fleeting instant what Lydia Kingston would say when they told her General really was a killer. She'd probably be delighted. So what if he'd killed the newspaper boy?

The black hound loomed over him, and Will rolled onto his stomach, trying to shield his face and neck with his arms. He could smell the hot feral breath and hear the angry threats of the dog's growl. Why didn't it go ahead and attack? What was it waiting for?

Will risked a quick look over his shoulder. He

couldn't believe what he saw. Old Buzzard Breath had the whole pack at bay. He stood close to Will's head, glowering at the others. The hound took a run at him, but the tan shepherd drove it back, nipping and barking, throwing the mongrel pack into total confusion.

They broke off their attack, moving in three different directions, the terrier yelping shrilly, the beagle mix with its tail between its legs. The black hound tried to circle and get behind the shepherd, but Buzzard Breath whirled, snapping at the hound's snarling muzzle, shouldering the dog down the hill.

Will scrambled to his feet. He could feel his breath coming in quick, frightened gasps. Forgetting the papers and his shoe, he ran, slipping and sliding on the gravel, up the hill.

A ridge of earth tripped him and sent him sprawling. He could feel the sting of gravel on his knees and see the blood where he had skinned the palms of his hands. There was a bark directly behind him. He turned, still on his knees, to face the big shepherd. Its massive, dirt-stained chest held the mark of old dried blood, from some other recent fight. His pointed muzzle was streaked with mud and his powerful haunches quivered, as though ready to spring. Or maybe they quivered from tiredness. Buzz abruptly sat down, his tongue lolling, his breath a rapid panting.

Will couldn't decide if he was seeing things or if Buzz's tail had just waved a friendly greeting. The big dog's jaws parted, so close to Will's own nose that it made him cross-eyed to look. Then, the big shepherd slurped his smooth, wet tongue across Will's chin and lips in one quick, decidedly friendly, motion.

"Thanks, hair ball."

Will was so relieved that his voice came out as a whisper. He cleared his throat and tried again. "You know, you just have regular doggy breath. No grosser than any other dog. Less gross than a lot of guys I know." Will reached over and scratched the fur on the shepherd's neck. Now that he was looking at the dog close up, it was kind of funny what a good-looking mutt he was. He was tan all over, with black on the tips of his ears and the tip of his tail. His legs faded as they went down so they were almost white at the bottom, and the thick hair on his underbelly was also a whitish tan color. If this dog's fur were on top of a girl's head, people would probably call it blond, and the guys would all wolf whistle at her.

Will, himself, whistled softly and Buzzard Breath crowded in close to him, panting. "Do you like that name? Buzzard Breath, I mean. It's what the kids call you, but if you don't like it, I can call you something else."

The dog looked at him, its dark eyes piercing the last of Will's defenses. "Look, I'm going to

call you Buzz. It's really not such a bad name."
Will hesitated and added, "It's a lot better than
Barfbrain."

Will got up and dusted off the seat of his jeans.
"I can't keep you if you follow me home, but I *can*
give you something to eat. Whaddaya say?"

Will took the wagging tail and the fact that the
dog was still there beside him as assent. "Help
me deliver the rest of these papers first, okay?"
He hobbled partway down the hill to pick up his
bag of newspapers and his shoe. "I need a body-
guard."

Buzz stuck with him for the twenty minutes it
took to finish the route. Will found himself talking to the dog about school, about David White,
about his slimebucket little brother, about everything that bothered him. Buzz was a great lis-
tener. Even better than Henry.

Henry and Max were waiting when Will and
Buzz got home. Henry was waiting–and Dave
White and a couple of the other guys were sitting
on their bikes in Will's driveway and ragging on
him. Dave rode a sleek black-and-red mountain
bike with wide, studded tires, and he twirled his
bike chain over his head like a cowboy's lariat.

"I've seen hot dogs bigger than that little
wiener of yours. Bet that dog's afraid you're
gonna swallow him for a snack, Biggenbottom.
How's that saying go? Big blubber, small dog?

Or is it cold nose, warm wienie?" David White was enjoying the laughter of the two guys lined up behind him. He showed no signs of stopping when he caught sight of Will and Buzz.

"Hey, here comes your best buddy, Biggenbottom. So, Wee Willie Winkle, what's up? Where'd you get that killer dog–no, wait, don't tell me. Omigod! You dognapped Buzzard Breath! Somebody call the fuzz. Hey, guys, it's the dog boys and their hounds of hell. Ooooo, I'm so scared."

"Hi, Henry." Will ignored the bully sitting in his driveway. His dad always told him that when you ignored somebody he'd eventually get tired of the game and go away. Unfortunately Will had never known this to hold true in real life. The bullies could dish it out far longer than he could take it. They must have bottomless buckets of bullyisms to draw from. He had a fairly short ration of patience.

Dave was twisting his bicycle chain in double loops, pulling it tight, letting it go, pulling it tight, letting it go. It was what Will's mom would call a nervous gesture, but it was hard to think of anything here that would make Dave nervous.

Buzz growled softly as he stood alertly beside Will. His ears were pricked forward and the hair on his back looked as if somebody had ruffled it backward. "Hey, Winkie-Dink, what's wrong with your wolf?"

Dave squared his boney shoulders and sent the bike chain whipping out in front of him like a weapon. It made a slight whistling noise as it cut through the air, slapping against his open palm with a sound as loud as a gunshot.

Buzz growled again, more loudly, and stalked a pace forward. "Easy, boy. Easy." Will reached down to stroke the shepherd's muzzle, but the dog flinched visibly as his hand passed over the scar above his nose. "It's okay." Will knelt down beside Buzz and ran his hand gently over the dog's snout, cupping it tenderly in his hands. Dogs couldn't talk. Not in words. But Buzz had as good as told him where that old scar came from. Someone, sometime in the past, had hit him with a whip.

"You better watch that dog. He's a mean one," Dave warned Will, his voice quickly changing to a boast. "Not that he scares me. I haven't met the dog yet I couldn't handle." The older boy whipped the bike chain against his palm a second time. Buzz suddenly lunged at him.

Will caught the black tip of the dog's tail and hung on, trying to hold Buzz back. Dave yelped, backing up so rapidly that he fell over backward with his bike on top of him. The rest of his gang wheeled around and headed for the street.

Dave scrambled to his feet, leaping onto his bike, and dropping the chain in his confusion. He shifted gears so sloppily that Will could hear them grinding into place, and then he was gone, chasing the others out onto the street with cries of "Wait for me, you bums!" and "That dog's crazy." Will had lost his grip on the shepherd's tail, and Buzz was right beside Dave now, nipping at his pedaling feet.

"Never met a dog he couldn't handle?" yelled Henry with a happy wink at Will. "Well, David White, meet Buzzard Breath. Or maybe we should call *you* David Yellow. Yeah! Blow it out your kazoo, Super Dork!"

Will looked at Henry with new respect. He hadn't known the little stamp collector had it in him.

Buzz disappeared down the street, barking at Dave's gang and nipping at all their flying feet. He was out of sight before Will picked up Dave's chain and chucked it in the metal garbage can, where it made a very satisfying clatter. But even though Will and Henry and Max sat around on the picnic bench in the side yard for half an hour, waiting for Buzz to return, the shepherd didn't come back.

"He'll be okay." Henry was trying to be reassuring, but Will had a funny feeling in his stomach.

"What if Dave hurt him?"

Henry looked at Will cross-eyed and stuck out his tongue.

"Okay, what if Dave told his parents and they put the dog catcher on him? What then?"

Henry nodded thoughtfully. "Yeah, that's a possibility. But what if he came back right now? What then? Would you keep him?"

Will didn't answer for several minutes. He was trying to twist a piece of grass into the letter *B*. He was also trying to think of an honest answer to Henry's question.

"Well?" Henry prodded. "He's not the kind of dog you've been saving up for, is he? I mean, don't get me wrong. I think he's great. Any dog who can make lunch meat out of Dave White is aces in my book. But he's just a regular old German shepherd, right? He's not the special dog you're looking for, is he?"

"No." Will said the word so softly that the sound of his mother's car coming up the driveway drowned it out. He tore the grass *B* into pieces and let them drop to the ground. "He's not the right dog for me. You're right. I just hope somebody gives him a good home."

"Hey, you can pet Max all you want until you get your own dog," offered Henry, and Max wagged his tail so hard that his small rump bumped back and forth with the effort.

"Time to set the table for dinner. Your friend can stay and eat with us if he wants," his mom yelled as she carried a bag of groceries into the kitchen. "And help me unload the car, Will."

"Coming," Will yelled back. Then he turned to Henry. "Even though Buzzard Breath isn't the right dog for me, he is my friend. That's all. He's just my friend, and I'm a little worried about him."

Henry nodded vigorously. "He's a great dog. He'll be fine, you'll see. So do you want me to stay for supper?"

"Yeah." Will grinned at him, suddenly glad Henry had come over. "At least I'll know where *one* of my friends is."

The Animal Shelter

The animal shelter stood far back from the road. It was a long, low cement-block building, painted a light green color that matched the washed-out green of the weedy grass field behind it. A big black sign with crisp white lettering hung from the six-foot-high chain-link fence that divided the shelter property from the large paved parking lot in front. The sign said: Notchcliff Humane Society.

After dinner Henry and Max had gone home, and a reluctant Bryan had come with Will and their dad to look around. It was one of Will's favorite things to do, even though he figured he wasn't likely to find his perfect dog here.

His perfect dog would be just like the feisty

terrier he'd seen on that old movie on TV last night. It didn't have to actually be a terrier. But it had to have a personality just like the dog in *The Proud Rebel*. Fiercely loyal. Hardworking. So smart that strangers would stop him in the street and ask, "How much do ya want for that dog a yourn, son?"

Then Will would smile, just like the kid in the old western, and say: "He's not for sale at any price, mister." That's how it would be when he found the perfect one-man dog–for whom he'd gladly be the perfect one-dog man.

In the meantime it was fun to look. The smell as they entered the shelter was a mixture of wet cement and antiseptic hospital odors, with an overlay of sour ammonia, almost a barnyard aroma that all the soap and disinfectant in the world couldn't quite mask.

On the right was the cat room, where tiny kittens and gray tabbies shared space in a five-level condo of boxy wood-and-mesh cages. On the left was a small office and a clinic area for flea dipping, deworming, and washing out cat pans. Through the lobby, in the back, was the kennel area, a long stretch of roomy wire-mesh pens, with swinging dog doors and outdoor runs. Mutts from poodle-spaniel mixes to black Labrador—collie combos lived here, next to purebred Irish setters ("he's a little too high-strung") and ancient basset hounds ("we can't keep him anymore, but we know you'll find him a wonderful home").

"Lookit!" Bryan shouted. "Lookit! Lookit!"

"Lookit what, dorkface?" asked Will, coming up behind his brother. He had to shout, too, to make himself heard over the deafening roar of excited barking that swept through the kennels as they slowly walked down the center aisle.

"Lookit, *Buzzard Breath!*" yelled Bryan, a pleased expression on his face. "Did you know he was in here? Wow! Old lady Kingston's killer pooch doesn't look so mean in a cage, now does he? In fact, you know what? I think he looks scared."

Will stopped in front of the narrow run where the dog paced restlessly up and down, up and down. Someone had finally removed that stupid pink scarf from around his neck. At first the big shepherd didn't seem to notice the boys.

"Hey, Buzzard Breath," taunted Bryan, bending over and putting a hand against the mesh. "How do ya like jail?"

"It's not a jail," Will protested. "It's a place for him to find a new family."

"For this handsome fellow I'm afraid it *is* a jail," said a gray-haired man in a white smock top and dark slacks, coming up behind Bryan and placing a hand on his shoulder. He looked at Will and shook his head sadly. "I'm afraid your friend here is right. In fact, it could be death row."

"I'm not his friend. I'm his brother," corrected Bryan, turning and reading the gold name tag pinned to the man's white top. "Do you work here—John?"

"Eleven and a half years. I'm the shelter medical technician. I clean 'em and feed 'em and haul 'em away when their time's up." John smiled at the boys. "Sometimes it's sad, but mainly I like the work."

"What do you mean by that death row stuff?" asked Will, facing the man who held a metal water dish in one hand and a wriggling brown puppy in the other.

"*This* is what people want," John answered, holding up the soft-furred creature that was so cute it looked almost like a stuffed toy. "They want *baby* dogs when they come in here to adopt. Hardly anybody's looking for older dogs. If they're more than five years old, it's almost sure to be the end of the line."

"But that's crazy," objected Will. "Buzzard Breath isn't old. And he didn't do anything wrong. There's no reason for him to be put to sleep."

"What's that you called him?" John asked, chuckling softly.

"It's just a nickname." Will flushed, embarrassed to find that a friend of his—a dog who'd saved his very life—could end up here, without a home, without a friend.

"Come here, son, take a look at this." The

sympathetic technician led the boys to an alcove where bags of dry dog food were piled on stainless steel counters. There was a newspaper article taped to the wall with the headline *The Unadoptables.*

"See, right here it says, at least seventy-five percent of dogs and cats over five never find a home. See these numbers? Last year we adopted two hundred fifty-nine dogs, out of the five hundred twenty dogs we took in. There were forty-five dogs adopted between the ages of two and five. There were two hundred three dogs under two. And there were eleven dogs over five. That's eleven, all total, out of five hundred twenty taken in. That's not very good odds, son."

"Buzz isn't old," Will protested.

"He's about five. We can tell by looking at the teeth."

"But you don't know," Will continued to protest. "You don't know that he couldn't be one of the eleven that *does* get adopted. He could be, couldn't he?"

"Well, son, I'd say his best chance, seeing as how you seem to care about him so much, is for *you* to adopt him."

Bryan, who had been letting the small brown puppy lick his fingers, slapped a hand to his forehead and began to giggle. "There you go, Will. Old Buzzard Breath's the *perfect* dog for you. I shoulda thought of it myself!"

Will walked back over to the shepherd's cage and stood, silently looking at his former enemy—and rescuer. The big tan dog was sitting forlornly in a corner of the enclosure, looking back at him. Was that a look of pleading in the dog's dark eyes? He didn't jump around or get excited the way the puppies and younger dogs did when anyone walked past their cages. He sat quietly. He was sort of dignified, thought Will.

He bent down and put his fingers on the mesh, and Buzz rose and came over to him, sniffing and tentatively thumping his tail. Will wondered what his dad would say if he asked to take this dog home.

But he couldn't do that. This wasn't his dream. Henry had been right about that. This was no *Proud Rebel* dog that people would admire and talk about. This was just . . .

"Buzzard Breath the Wonder Dog! I bet you'll never find a better match for your dorky personality," needled Bryan, coming up behind him.

For once his bratty brother was right. He couldn't take Buzzard Breath home. He couldn't give up on his dream dog.

But what if John was right, too? He couldn't let Buzz die, either. Could he?

Decision

"Hi there, son! You're getting to be a regular out here. Maybe we should put you to work!" John motioned to Will from the spot where he was rolling up the heavy orange hose after spraying down the kennel floor. Puddles of water still stood, like tiny flat lakes, caught in invisible dips in the gray cement floor of the center aisle.

"Just checking by. On the tan shepherd. How's he doing?" asked Will. "Did you find him a home yet?"

Will had been asking the same question every day for the past five days. Every time he asked it, he wasn't sure if he wanted to hear a "yes" or a "no." Oh, he wanted Buzzard Breath safely settled in a new home, but he didn't want him stuck with another owner like Mrs. Kingston.

"He's still here," replied John with a grin. "In fact, I think he's been waiting for you."

Will knelt down beside the cage and pulled an Oreo cookie out of his pocket, offering it to Buzz between the wires. It was the same thing he'd brought every day, five times in a row. The shepherd took it daintily from his fingers. Some days the cookie treat left black crumbs in his blond fur, but today Buzz seemed to swallow it whole.

"So, this is gonna be the big day," said John, coming up behind him, still grinning.

"Whaddaya mean?" asked Will, looking up at the friendly shelter technician.

"You know. The day you take this one home with you."

"No." Will paused as the grin seemed to fall off John's face. "I want Buzz—General—to find the *right* family. But I'm savin' up for a purebred dog. You know, a registered dog with papers. I'm just visiting Buzz until he gets his real family."

"Well, son"—John's expression had become serious, almost stern—"his time here is up today. I thought you knew that. If you, or somebody, don't take him today, we'll have to be putting him down after adoption hours this afternoon."

"Today? But he hasn't been here very long. Not even a whole week. You haven't really given him a chance," Will protested.

John's expression softened slightly. "Yeah, well, maybe someone will come in and adopt him tonight. There's always hope. But we've got a big backlog of dogs right now. We keep every dog for at least five days, and sometimes, if we have the room, we keep them longer. But things are crowded right now. Lots of new puppies. And I did tell ya, son, remember, the first night you came, that these older dogs don't usually *find* homes. I thought for sure *you'd* decide to take him before it was too late."

Will had no answer. He was thinking. He needed a plan. He'd been trying to think of one, but it looked as if his thinking time was just about up. Any plan would do; it didn't even have to be a good one.

"Okay. Let's see. If I took him home with me, I could take him back to Mrs. Kingston and see if maybe she missed him. . . ." He was thinking out loud now, but as soon as he said the words he knew that was a terrible plan. Mrs. Kingston had Bathsheba. She was a cat person. Besides, she had a new guard dog. Will had met Assassin last Saturday when he went over to mow the lawn. Now, there was a dog who was seriously mean.

"No, that won't work. Okay. Maybe if I took him home, I could find him a new family myself. My folks said they're ready for a dog anytime I'm ready, as long as I take care of him." Will's expression grew determined. "So that's what I'll do. I'll take care of Buzz. I can ask my friends. I can make signs and put them up on telephone poles."

"Signs?" John sounded doubtful.

"Yeah. You know. 'Great Dog Free to Good Family.'"

"Don't you have a good family, son?"

"Sure. It's not that. It's just that I know what kinda dog I want, and this one isn't it. He's not the perfect dog for me. But I still don't want to see him put to sleep."

"How do ya know he's not the dog for you until you take him home and give him a chance?" asked John, his face expressionless now.

"I just know," answered Will, not paying much attention to the old man with the mop. "But . . ." He paused and then blurted out the words. "I'm gonna do it. I really am. I'm gonna take him home with me today. I'll just keep him till I find him a good home. It'll be a temporary thing. So, John, how do I do this? What do I do to take him home?"

"Mr. Snavely will take care of you in the front office." John pointed down the aisle to the lobby. Will jumped up and hurried in that direction. Now that he'd made the decision he wanted to get things rolling.

"So what do ya think, old fella?" asked John,

rubbing the shepherd's snout as it pressed against the mesh. "Can you turn into the 'perfect dog' for that boy of yours?" John was watching Will's retreating back as he turned into the office. "Or will you end up back here with old John before too long? I'm right glad that boy's decided to take a chance on you." John turned and clicked his tongue encouragingly at Buzzard Breath. "I just hope he decides to keep you."

The Perfect Dog

Will wanted a dog that would impress the other guys. It couldn't be an ordinary dog.

Old Buzzard Breath was ordinary. He was a common German shepherd. Plain tan. Half the people in the world had dumb old German shepherds.

Sure, Buzz could do a few tricks. He could heel and stay and roll over, and he could even catch a Frisbee if you didn't throw it too high. Dave White himself had come over for a closer look when he was riding past and saw their game of catch. Dave bragged that his uncle was a policeman and had a German shepherd that could catch crooks.

"I guess we already know old Buzzard Breath

is a rotten guard dog." Dave had been standing outside Will's fenced-in side yard when he said that. "After my dad called the dogcatcher the guy didn't have hardly any trouble catching this one. He rounded up that whole pack of strays in the woods, and they all gave him a hard time except this wimp."

So it had been Dave. The anger rose in Will's throat every time he thought of it, like the sour taste of scalded milk.

"He knew enough to chase you," Will replied sharply.

But he had to grudgingly admit that Buzz wasn't a good guard dog. If he had been, Lydia Kingston wouldn't have dumped him. He wouldn't have ended up at the shelter. Will wouldn't have been out the $28.50 adoption fee just because he couldn't stand to see a dumb dog put to sleep. He'd be $28.50 closer to the dog he *really* wanted.

Will stretched out on his bed, thumbing through the library's brand new edition of the *American Kennel Club Complete Dog Book*. Buzz lay on the floor in front of him, looking up every now and then and thumping his tail against the floorboards. That proves he's a dumb dog, thought Will. There's a rug out in the living room. He'd be more comfortable on a rug.

Buzz looked up at him again and rolled over on his back, obviously inviting Will to rub his stomach.

"Dumb dog," said Will, reaching down to ruffle his hand through the soft yellowish fur as Buzz rumbled with pleasure. "You sound like a cat, you dumb old dog. Stop your purring or I'll start calling you Kitty Whiskers." Buzz continued his deep-throated growl of contentment.

"Would you like it better if I called you General?" Will's fingers traced a maze of circles on the dog's powerful chest. "Mrs. Kingston called you General. But I like Buzzard Breath better. It sounds more like you. It suits you. It's a good name for a dumb old dog with dog-food breath. If I could register you with the American Kennel Club, your name could be Winkle's Buzzard Breath of Notchcliff. How'd you like that?" Will laughed at his own joke. "I'd sure like to hear some announcer saying *that* at a dog show."

Will pulled his hand away, ignoring Buzz's forlorn whine. "Except *you'll* never be in any dog show. You're just an old mutt that nobody wants."

Will opened the book to a spot about halfway through and whistled appreciatively. "*This* is what I'm going to get. Take a look at this."

He turned the book around to show Buzz a picture of a tan-colored dog with pointed, erect ears, a deep black muzzle, and a thick curling tail. He pulled the book back up onto the bed and began to read out loud: "The Akita is designated as a national monument in his native country of Japan. He is a larger-sized descendant of the ancient Oriental dog whose likeness has been found carved in the tombs of these early Japanese people. This breed is a wonderful combination of dignity, good nature, alert courage and docility."

"And he's good-lookin', too. Especially compared to you." Will reached down and pulled up on Buzz's muzzle so the dog was looking him straight in the eye. "So where's your 'courage and docility,' huh?" Buzz's sad brown eyes were intent on Will's face. His tail wagged back and forth like a furry flag.

"Just what I thought. You don't have any." Will rolled over onto his back, holding the book up over his head and flipping the pages until he found another picture he liked.

"How about this one?" he asked, rolling back over, and showing Buzz a photograph of a big, long-haired black-and-white dog with long floppy ears and a long droopy tail. "This is a Bernese mountain dog. See? It says it was brought into Switzerland over two thousand years ago by invading Roman soldiers. See the word they use to describe it? 'Aristocratic.' I bet nobody ever called you aristocratic."

Will let the book slide to the floor as Buzz licked his hand up one side and down the other. "Hey, cut that out!"

Will pulled his hand away, but one bare foot still dangled over the side of the bed. Buzz shifted to it and began carefully to lick the ticklish bottom of the foot. Will giggled. The dog's rough tongue felt funny. It felt kind of nice, actually. He looked over at Buzz, who had stopped licking and was looking at Will expectantly. The only trouble was, after a dog was done licking your feet it was like when he finished licking another dog's coat. He looked at you as though he expected you to lick him back.

Will flipped over, ignoring Buzz but still talking to him. "That's what I want. Something 'aristocratic.' Something unusual. something nobody else has. I want a dog I can really be proud of." He grabbed Buzz's snout and rolled off the bed onto the floor, mock wrestling the dog across the smooth pine boards.

"If I had a dog like that, I'd call it Warrior. You hear that? It would be a fighter, a champion." Will scooped up the book and bounced back up onto the bed as he heard his father's steps coming down the hall. "I can't call you Warrior," he whispered as he reached over to click off the light. "Or even General. Buzzard Breath is the only name that fits, you, you dumb old dog."

The bedroom door opened and Will could see the outline of his father's head. "Lights out in here?" His dad spoke into the darkness. "Good. Now, go to sleep. Remember, Will, you're substituting on that morning newspaper route again tomorrow, so you'd better get some rest." There was a pause. "Is that dog in here?"

"He's right here. Beside the bed."

"Well, you can keep him on the floor in your room for now. But if he makes a mess or if he makes it hard for you to get to sleep, we'll put him out in the garage. He'll do just fine out there. Believe me. Dogs like places like that."

"No, it's okay. He'll behave. Good night, Dad."

"Good night, son. Sleep tight."

Darkness swallowed the room when his father shut the door. Will waited until he heard his dad's footsteps walking away. Then he reached out and turned the small light beside his bed back on.

"Come on, Buzz. Come up here." He patted the bed beside him. The dog didn't need any more urging. He gathered his feet under him and leaped up, landing on Will's legs and flopping around in a tangle of sheets and feet. Will patted the space beside him. "Here," he repeated.

Buzz snuggled up beside him as Will reopened the dog book, turning to the table of contents. He ran his finger down the page, whispered, "Two hundred sixty-eight," and turned to the proper section. He read silently in the stillness of the room.

"Derived from the old breeds of herding and farm dogs, and associated for centuries with man as a servant and companion, the German shepherd is first, last, and all the time, a working dog. Working with police, with the armed services, and as a guide dog for the blind, the shepherd has endeared itself to a wide public in practically every country of the globe as a protector and friend. In his relation to man, he does not give affection lightly: he has plenty of dignity and some suspicion of strangers. But his friendship, once given, is given for life."

Will looked down at the tan dog with its broad forehead, its black nose half tucked under his shoulder, its eyes closed, and its pointed, black-tipped ears relaxed. He closed the book, putting it on the table beside the lamp as he reached to turn the light out once more.

"For life, huh? Well, I sure won't have you that long," he whispered softly. Buzz's bushy black-tipped tail thumped three times against the bed. "What would I want with a dumb old Buzzard Breath, anyway?" Will settled against his pillow, his left arm encircling the dog's neck. He felt Buzz's cold nose against his cheek. The dog's breathing was deep and even, his body warm and comfortable.

"No way," Will sighed softly, drifting off to sleep. "Maybe a week more. But that's all."

Doodling

Will doodled a spiral and a linked chain of triangles across the top of a blank sheet of paper. He was watching a golf tournament on TV with his dad, and it was sort of boring. He liked baseball and *Wrestlemania* a lot better.

Will still hadn't decided on the perfect name for the dog he'd be getting when he'd saved enough money. Buzz had only cost $28.50, so he didn't have to save up much money to get his bank account back to where it'd been. Of course, he'd find Buzz a good home by the time he got his real dog.

He couldn't have two dogs at the same time. His parents had told him that. So he'd have to find Buzz the perfect owner, while he was finding himself the perfect dog.

The shepherd lay between his legs on the floor, sound asleep. Will figured golf did that to you—put you to sleep—even if you were a dog.

Will was sprawled on the carpet and Buzz's head rested companionably on his rear end, so it was hard to tell where Will left off and Buzz began.

Maybe he'd get a magnificent bullmastiff. Or maybe a blue-eyed Siberian husky, thought Will, doodling names as he daydreamed. He'd seen giggling girls in school doodle the names of boys they liked on their notebook covers. As for him, he liked dogs.

HERCULES. FALCONER. WOLFGANG. WARRIOR. Will wrote the names in boxy block letters. It had to be a grand name, a magnificent name, a name that fit perfectly.

BUZZ. BUZZ. BUZZ. He didn't know why, but the shepherd's silly name rolled off his pen again and again. BUZZARD BREATH. B-BREATH. BUZZMAN. BUZZ.

Buzz's ears twitched, and his head shifted, seeking a softer spot on Will's anatomy. Will heard his father make a noise that sounded like a snort and whistle, and he looked over to see his dad's head tilted forward, eyes closed, and lips parted in another raspy snore. The golf tournament had even put his father to sleep, thought Will with a slow smile. And his dad played golf.

Will pressed his legs more tightly around

Buzz's solid body and sketched a big *B* with a little *u* snuggled up against it and a long row of *z*'s marching beside it.

"Fore!" called a voice from the TV, and there was a *wap* and a soft oohing sound from the crowd at greenside.

Will's fingers moved absently over the paper. B-U-

He was still doodling *z* when he, too, fell asleep.

One Nice Thing About Dogs

Slime."

"What did you call me, runt?"

"I didn't call you nothin', butthead. But you're drinking slime."

"I'm drinking a chocolate milk shake." Will made a loud slurping noise and licked his lips. "And I'm not letting you taste it, either. You'd suck up the whole thing."

"I wouldn't touch it." Bryan wrinkled his nose in distaste. "It's made with slime."

"You're crazy."

"Methylcellulose. They use methylcellulose to thicken fast-food milk shakes. It's the drippy stuff they put on aliens in horror movies to make 'em yucky. I read about it in *Monster Magic Magazine*."

"You're crazy," Will repeated. He took a sip of the creamy-looking milk shake, but an uninvited vision of glistening green skin flashed through his head, and he swallowed with difficulty.

He looked down at Buzz. The tan shepherd was watching him eagerly, always alert for a possible treat when Will was eating. Will bent down, tilting the big paper cup so Buzz could reach the bottom with his tongue. "Besides which, I always share stuff like this with Buzz."

"You share slime with your dog?" asked Bryan in mock amazement.

"Buzz wouldn't eat it if it were slime," snorted Will, looking down at the milk shake cup.

"Are you kidding? Slime is probably Buzzard Breath's favorite dish!"

Will belched, turning his head toward his little brother in hopes of spraying him with hot, icky breath. But Bryan dodged around the corner and down the hall, yelling, "Gross! You're a gross geek sundae with dog poop on top!"

"You're a mutant milk shake with vomit on the side," Will called after him, satisfied that he'd held his own and maybe even won the ongoing contest to be more disgusting than his brother.

Buzz licked the big paper milk shake cup clean and lay on his belly, looking hopefully at Will, tail wagging slowly.

"Nope. That's it." Will held up his empty hands to convince the big dog there was no more. He lay down beside Buzz on the living room floor, using the dog's back as a pillow. Will propped his feet up on the couch and twisted to reach for the report card that was mixed with that day's pile of mail by his dad's chair. He felt a bubble of gas ready to pop and lifted one leg for a satisfying and disgusting toot. After all, he had to work at staying champion.

Buzz yawned and laid his head on his paws.

That was one nice thing about dogs, thought Will. They didn't care when you made disgusting noises. They didn't even seem to notice. You could have underarm odor and bad breath and a dog would still like you. Everyone in the whole school could think you were weird and a brain and try to avoid you, but a dog would still like you.

Will unfolded and read his report card for the third time. Straight A's. Parents liked it when you got straight A's, thought Will, looking at his report card. It was part of the deal he had with his dad. He needed good grades to keep a dog. But it wasn't something you told the guys about.

Sometimes Will wondered if it was worth it, being smart. If you didn't handle it right, dumb kids treated you like a nerd, and popular kids wanted to copy your homework in exchange for the chance to hang out with them for ten minutes. Sometimes Will wondered if he'd be happier if he were a little more stupid.

And that was another thing dogs seemed glad to overlook. They didn't care if you were a retard or an Einstein clone. In fact, Will realized, whenever he tried to puzzle out just what it was about people that dogs liked, he always came up blank.

After all, most animals stayed far away from people. Unless you were a veterinarian or a zookeeper or Michael Jackson, you couldn't even touch a giraffe or a chimpanzee. Even common animals, like squirrels and chipmunks, always scurried out of reach. But dogs sat right down on your feet, looked you in the eye, and were always happy to see you. Even when you pulled their ears over their eyes like a blindfold. Even when you took their paws and made them wave and do arm gestures like an opera singer. Even when you forgot to give them fresh water.

Will didn't understand *why* dogs liked people. People didn't really do anything to deserve to be liked by dogs. But there it was.

Of course, not *all* dogs liked *all* people. Look at Buzz and Dave White. Will tossed his report card back onto the pile of mail for his dad to see when he got home from work, then rolled over onto his stomach. "You like *almost* everybody, though, don't ya, boy? That guard-dog stuff at Mrs. Kingston's house was just a big act, wasn't it?" Will took Buzz's furry snout in one cupped hand

and put his own nose against the dog's cold, dark one.

"Have you seen that monster she has now?" Will whistled softly, making Buzz's tail beat more quickly. "He's something else. He looks a little bit like you, except he's all black, with tan patches on his rump and chest. And he's M-E-E-A-A-N." Will drew the word out for emphasis. He shifted Buzz's cold nose to his cheek. "That dog doesn't just growl, he snarls. He acts like he's hungry and he thinks people are big, juicy T-bone steaks. Mrs. Kingston says she got him from her brother-in-law, the one who has that farm you came from. The one who raises attack dogs."

Will liked the way Buzz's nose felt against this cheek, but he yelled and jumped up when the shepherd's long tongue shot out and slurped across his ear.

"Yuck. Dog kisses. P-U," he teased, catching at the air in front of Buzz's snout in the familiar game of keep-away. It had been four weeks since Buzz had come for his temporary visit. Will hadn't meant to keep him so long, but there was school and the newspaper route and hanging out with Henry and, of course, his perfect-dog research. He was a busy guy. He hadn't found time to put up posters or put an ad in the paper to find Buzz a new home. Not yet, anyway.

"I gotta go to school—just for an hour or so.

I'm supposed to help Mrs. Ludke pack books and sweep out for the summer. So you can go off exploring on your own for a little while," suggested Will, banging open the screen door and grabbing a can of soda on his way out. "But stay away from Mrs. Kingston and her new dog. I hear its name is Assassin. That sounds pretty mean to me. Even meaner than your old name. Okay, maybe it's more dignified than Buzzard Breath. But think about it. You're Buzz for short. That's what everybody calls you. So what's that dog's nickname?!"

Will's mother rushed past them and climbed into their big gray VW van, motioning Will to the passenger side. "I'm running late again, but I can drop you at the school if you hurry."

Will winked at Buzz and gave him a last scratch between the ears. "See ya later, sport. You can help me deliver the papers." The screen door banged shut behind him but didn't click.

As the car pulled away, Buzz pressed his snout against the screen and it swung open easily. He trotted down the driveway behind the car and stood watching it disappear down Spring Garden Street.

He stood in that same expectant position, waiting for Will to return, for three long minutes. Then, with a low whine of disappointment, he turned and headed back up the driveway and into the woods beyond, pausing once when a car roared by on the nearby street. There was no other noise. No sign of Will.

So Buzz continued uphill, vanishing in the shadows cast by a stand of tall, leafy maples.

Framed

At first the sound didn't register. The thin, high-pitched scream sounded like a hundred little kids screaming in a hundred backyards, fighting with their brothers and sisters over a hundred silly toys. Buzz didn't usually pay much attention to such irritating human noises.

But as he wandered slowly in the direction of the sound, exploring a fresh rabbit trail here and a groundhog burrow there, a new note was added to the discordant wail. It was a noise made by a dog, and it instantly roused Buzz's curiosity. He tested the air for a long minute, trying to read the story behind the sounds.

There was a sharp, acrid odor of fear—a familiar human scent that always made him edgy.

And there was something else. A feral smell full of rage and triumph.

Buzz walked down the hill slowly, testing the air. Whatever was happening, it was happening near the woman's house—the place where he used to live—and Buzz hesitated, unsure if he wanted to get any closer. Another, less familiar, smell reached him on a hint of summer breeze, then blew past to the other curious noses in the woods.

It was the ripe, musky odor of blood.

Buzz began to lope down the hill, tail held stiffly behind him, hackles rising. He growled softly as he approached the two figures on either side of the white picket fence beside Mrs. Kingston's house.

The child, a two-year-old girl with wispy red curls all over her head, sat beside the fence, one arm stuck through the slats. A black shepherd, bigger than Buzz, stood stiff-legged on the other side of the fence, his jaws clamped on the girl's arm, an ugly snarl rumbling in his throat. Blood dripped from his muzzle.

The girl's freckles stood out darkly across the bridge of her nose, making her pale face look ghostly white. A string of spittle hung from her open mouth, puddling on her red T-shirt as her frantic wail rose and fell. Her other arm beat weakly against the fence. Assassin, with that distinctive tan mark on his rump, was braced firmly against her feeble tugging. His black eyes were angry slits, his thin black lips curving back to reveal cruel teeth.

Loud rock music blared from the windows of the brick house behind the child, the drum beat adding a primitive rhythm to the savage scene.

Buzz barked once, stalking a wide U around the two figures. Neither yard was fully fenced in. The decorative picket fencing, like the wooden latticework under Lydia Kingston's porch, was simply "for show."

The chewed, frayed end of a rope hung limply from Assassin's leather collar. A blue rubber ball lay against the fence on the dog's side, resting where it had rolled after the child dropped it.

The girl's screaming grew louder as she caught sight of Buzz. The sound was starting to hurt his sensitive ears. Buzz had to stop this child's screams. The smell of blood guided him, telling him what he had to do. He must make Assassin let go.

Standing beside the little girl, Buzz pressed his snout through the slats and began to bark. It was a warning bark, a deep, full-throated, commanding bark, that broached no argument. Assassin's snarl softened, trailing off into a confused growl. Buzz barked again, thumping his body against the fence this time. The little girl's shrill, stuttering screams never stopped.

Suddenly the black dog dropped the girl's arm

and backed up a step, keeping his eyes fixed on Buzz. He began to bark in answer, a cowardly bark that, if you listened closely, sounded like an insistent: "Not me. It wasn't me. I didn't do it."

The sound of a door slamming open sent Assassin, tail between his legs, bounding around the corner of the porch to disappear underneath it. The blackness under the porch was like a blotter, hungrily absorbing the black dog. It was as if he'd never even been there.

Buzz nosed the arm of the sobbing child gently. Through gasping, hiccoughing sobs, she choked out the words: "Doggie hurt me." She let Buzz lick her wound, then looked at his blood-stained snout and began to wail all over again.

A teenage girl, sprinting around the brick house with a portable phone clutched in her hand, lent her own screams to the child's wails as she came closer. She stopped short and spoke urgently into the phone.

"Oh my god, Frank. Anita's been attacked by a vicious dog. *That's* where she got to while we were talking. She's bleeding and the dog's standing over her right here in the front yard! What should I do?!"

There was a brief second of silence while the girl listened to the voice on the other end of the phone, and the child caught her breath. Then the wailing resumed, and the girl said, "Yes! Call 911. Tell them to hurry!"

She advanced on Buzz, holding the antenna of the phone out like a sword in front of her. Suddenly she whipped the thin metal antenna across Buzz's nose. There was a hiss of air and a sharp snap when metal met flesh.

Buzz yelped and scrambled away from the mad woman who yelled and waved her arms at him; she hit him again, this time on his rump. He struggled to keep his footing as he backed away from the girl, but fell over and begged, belly up, for her to end this unwarranted attack. Instead the teenager brought the silvery antenna down on his upturned stomach, and he yelped again, rolling into a more protected position.

The sound of sirens, an echo of the little girl's reedy wail, cut through the hot morning air. The child had finally stopped crying to watch, wide-eyed, as her baby-sitter attacked Buzz with the whip-like portable phone antenna. The tan shepherd had almost reached the end of the fence, just a short leap to the relative safety of the woods, when an ambulance, a medic unit, and a police car screamed up to the curb by the front sidewalk.

As his teenage tormenter turned to meet the rescue crew, Buzz sprang to his feet and ran, full out, for the nearby trees.

"Get him! Stop him!" he heard her yell behind him. "He attacked the baby. He was standing over her, about to kill her, when I heard him barking. I ran out just in time to save her. I held him off with this."

"Calm down, Miss. Just calm down." This voice was deeper, full of authority. "We'll catch the dog soon enough. You're sure that's the one? The one that just ran off?"

"Oh yes. That's the one, Officer. The tan shepherd. I only turned my back for a minute, and Anita got out the door, and the dog jumped right over the fence and tried to kill her. I had to pull him off. I was scared he'd kill me too, and then . . ."

"Yes, yes, it must have been quite a shock." The deep, calm voice interrupted her. "But you say you *saw* the whole thing? Can you describe the dog? Did he have any distinguishing marks?"

"He was tan. Tan all over. Except his ears and the tip of his tail. They were black. And I left a big red welt across his nose when I hit him."

"Good. That's good. We'll find him—soon— and lock him up. You can rest easy on that score, miss."

"Thank you, Officer. I can't bear to think what might have happened if I hadn't gotten here so quickly. You've got to catch that dog, Officer. You've got to put that monster to sleep. He's a killer."

Presumed Guilty

Will was so sad that his face felt stiff. He wanted to cry. His eyes ached to cry. His cheeks and his forehead felt as if somebody had poured cement into them, painfully stiffening them into one blank expression. His voice sounded flat and strained to his own ears, and much older than it ever had before.

His mother explained it and then explained it again. She'd even turned cartoons on, allowing TV without once asking if his chores were done. She'd answered all his questions and even cooked his favorite dinner of cheeseburgers and curly fries. But none of it made him feel any better.

Buzz was gone.

And even though Bryan the Brat reminded him that he hadn't planned on keeping Buzz forever anyway, and that he could get that great new dog he wanted now—well, it still boiled down to the same thing. Buzz was gone. And Will felt awful.

Anyway, it hardly seemed fair that the cops came while he wasn't even home. He'd only been at school for a few hours, to sort textbooks and wash blackboards for Mrs. Ludke. Jeez, it was the beginning of summer. After today he'd been planning to spend all his newfound free time finding Buzz a home. Just being with Buzz.

But Buzz was gone.

His mom said two cops in a black-and-white squad car, followed by a khaki-colored Animal Control van, pulled into their driveway at 3 p.m. They'd come for Buzz.

They'd asked around the neighborhood for a big tan shepherd with just a little black on his ears and tail. And someone had pointed them right to this house and Buzz.

His mother told him how she'd held Buzz's collar as he growled, then barked, then growled again at the three men who stood together just inside the kitchen door.

One of the policemen had a paper—something signed by a judge—saying Buzz had to be turned over to the authorities. He had to be tested for rabies. To insure the safety of the community. It didn't actually say he had to be killed. But Will knew that's what it meant.

His mother said that Buzz seemed to know something was wrong. But he let her put the leather muzzle the Animal Control officer handed her over his snout and buckle it behind his ears. The policemen had apologized and listened politely when she argued with them. But they obviously hadn't believed his mother when she protested that Buzz didn't bite that little girl. That Buzz would never bite anybody.

They never even looked for another dog. For the guilty dog. They just came and got Buzz.

"Who are their witnesses? Who are they?" asked Will desperately.

"Well, one is the little girl who got bitten. But she's only two. The policeman said she cried when they showed her a picture of a German shepherd like Buzz." His mother repeated the conversation for Will, word for word.

"She cried when we showed her a picture like your German shepherd," said the first cop.

"Yeah, but she cried when we showed her a picture of a stuffed poodle. She even cried when we showed her a picture of Garfield the cat," said the other cop.

"Okay, well, she's not our best witness," said the first. "But there's also"—he checked a small notebook that he pulled from his back pants pocket—"a Mrs. Kingston. Her brother-in-law provided us with most of the facts when he came down to the station. He said this"—the officer paused and checked his notebook again—"Mrs. Kingston heard a terrible racket and came out on her porch to see what was happening. He said there was a big German shepherd attacking the little girl who lived next door."

"But what about *her* dog?" Will's mom had asked. "She has her own German shepherd. Did he tell you that? Maybe she was trying to protect her own dog."

"We didn't see any dog, ma'am. Just a . . ." The policeman again consulted the small lined steno pad in his hand. "Just a cat. Name of Bathsheba. Big yellow cat. Guard cat, she called it. Though I don't think I've ever heard of a cat called such a thing before." He looked at his partner for confirmation. But the other policeman was already helping the animal-control officer pull Buzzard Breath into the waiting van.

"She does, too, have a dog!" Will interrupted his mother's story. "She calls him Assassin, just like she used to call Buzz General. She even told me Assassin is a better dog. But he's not. He's just mean."

"The policeman said they had *another* witness, too," his mother continued. "The child's baby-sitter saw the whole thing. That's three witnesses–or at least two, Will. I don't know how we can fight that. Your father is checking with a lawyer.

But he doesn't hold out much hope."

"Where'd they take Buzz?" asked Bryan, jumping into the conversation for the first time. "To the slammer? Did they take him to the Big House? Is he a convict dog now?"

"You can't be a convict if you haven't been convicted. And you can't be convicted if you haven't had a trial," argued Will.

"Unfortunately, sweetheart, I'm not sure it works that way for dogs," said his mother. "They may be presumed guilty unless *proven* innocent."

"We could help him bust out," Bryan offered. "Like they do in the prison movies." Bryan was making enthusiastic plans, oblivious of his big brother's mood. "We could tunnel under the wall, or maybe we could slip him a file, or smuggle him out in the laundry bin!"

"They took Buzz to the animal shelter, dear," said their mother calmly. "I don't think they have laundry at the shelter."

"It's not fair!" shouted Will, suddenly, unreasonably angry. He wasn't really angry at his mother or even his brother. They were just the only ones there.

"It's a terrible thing to happen to Buzz–and to you," his mother agreed sympathetically, placing a hand on his shoulder. "And I can't imagine that Buzz would ever do what they say he did. But with all those witnesses, I don't see that there's anything we can do, Will. Your dad says what we should really worry about now is our own liability, for letting the dog out without a leash. He hopes we're covered by our homeowner's policy."

She stopped talking, absorbing the grim look on Will's face. Then she tried changing the subject. "Hey, your father promised you can go look at some new puppies tonight. Maybe tonight you'll find the dog you *really* want."

"No!" Will slammed his fist against the table, ignoring the pain. The pain felt good. "Buzz is the dog I really want." He headed for the screen door. His bike was parked just outside. He'd paid fifty-five dollars out of his savings for a total realignment, a new tire and tube, and even a new gearshift chain.

Will hit the kickstand so hard with his foot that the bike fell over with a crash. He picked it up angrily and climbed on.

"Where are you going?" asked his mother.

"What about the papers?" asked Bryan.

"I've got something I have to do." Will didn't look back. Maybe Buzz wouldn't have a trial and a lawyer. But he'd have a chance, if Will could help it.

It was his job to give Buzz that chance.

Death Row

That's my dog."

"This's nobody's dog, son. This here is a canine crim-i-nal and he's about to pay his debt to so-ci-e-ty." The animal warden drawled his words, as if he enjoyed the sound of them. "So you best get on home. This in't gonna be somethin' you'll be wantin' ta watch."

"He *is* my dog," Will repeated stubbornly. "And he shouldn't be here. There's been a terrible mistake. You've got the wrong dog."

"We don't make no mistakes, son. The only mistake here is the one this dog made when he attacked that poor little girl. Now, I'm gonna ask you agin to get on home. And the next time I asks ya, I won't be so perlite."

"But . . ."

"Out. I mean O-U-T, boy. Git going." The man in the khaki jacket wore a name tag, just like John's. Only this one said Ed. Will had seen him around during those five days Buzz was first at the shelter. He mopped floors and washed out cat pans. Apparently he also served as official dogcatcher.

Will turned back to Buzz. His hands were balled up into fists, and he felt like he had to hit something or bust. He slammed a hand into one of the metal posts that held the wire mesh of the dog runs. The post didn't even vibrate. But it hurt his hand. A lot.

An unwelcome wave of tears washed into Will's eyes, but he blinked them back. Buzz looked up at him trustingly. His shaggy tail thumped against the cement of the gray kennel floor, and he crowded closer to the wire that separated him from Will.

"Don't worry, boy. I'll get you out of here. I'll think of something," Will whispered, extending his fingers until they touched the shepherd's cold black nose.

"Hey! Watch that! That dog'll bite yer hand off iffen you're not careful." The warden's tone softened slightly. "I know you hate to see a handsome dog like this one put down, but, believe me, son, it's the only way. Once they go bad, they stay that way. Believe me, that devil would gladly bite your hand off if you gave him half a chance. So go on home, boy. Git along."

Will ignored Ed's stupid advice and jammed his fingers through the mesh. He caressed Buzz's grizzled chin. He could feel the old whipping scar, and now there was a new ridge of scar tissue, forming a spidery X on the dog's snout. Will knew the new scar had been made by a teenage girl wielding a wire telephone antenna. It looked like a mark of guilt. It looked like an open-and-shut case.

"Yeah. Okay. I'm going. But I'm telling you, you've got the wrong dog. And I mean to prove it."

"Well, you'd better hurry up and find that proof, son. And you better run right back here with it. The office'll be closed when we're working in the back this afternoon, and you'll just get one of them answer machines. And by the time anybody hears your message, it'll probably be too late. 'Cause this fellow's scheduled for a lethal injection this afternoon. The vet tech will be here to do it. After that, all that'll be left is a few pieces of bone in the incinerator." It was obvious Ed enjoyed talking about these grisly details. It was obvious Ed liked his work.

"I'll be back," Will promised again, his stomach twisting into a tight knot of fear. "Buzz didn't do anything wrong. You'll see. You've got the wrong dog."

Lawyer for the Defense

Sometimes things didn't seem so exciting when you were doing them. Like being on vacation. Will could be at the beach with only his parents and Bryan to hang out with. He could be body-surfing and digging in the sand and eating soft custard on the boardwalk. All ordinary beach stuff. Nothing great.

But then when he was back in school, remembering vacation, the memories were always wonderful. Will had never understood why that happened.

Until now.

Will knew now that things aren't always clear until you look *back* at them. When you're in the middle of things they can get confusing. But when you have a clear view, when you have what his dad called "perspective," it all became so simple. It was hard to believe that you'd ever missed it in the first place.

He'd thought of Buzz as just a temporary dog. Buzz wasn't the pedigreed, high-class breed he wanted to own. That dog would be something special. It would play with him and listen to him and love him.

Just like Buzz. That dog *was* Buzz.

There was nothing temporary about it. Will *had* to find a way to save Buzz, and the only way he could think of required a visit to Lydia Kingston.

Something else had gotten clearer lately, too. Henry had volunteered to come with him to see Mrs. Kingston. Wimpy little Henry. David White had put caps under Henry's chair one day last week. They'd gone off with a loud bang when Henry sat down, and he'd jumped so high the kids had laughed about it for the rest of the day. Even Will had laughed.

But now, when it came to something really scary, like standing up to Dragon Lady Kingston, Henry offered to stand beside him.

Of course, when the two of them were standing on Mrs. Kingston's porch, backed up against the rail, trying not to look nervous as they waited for her to come to the door, Henry did stand *behind* Will. But it felt good not to be here alone.

Lydia Kingston had Bathsheba in her arms when she came to the door. "If you're lookin' around for that killer dog, he's gone," she said as both boys stretched up on their toes, trying to look over her shoulder and see if the black shepherd was behind her. "Howie come and took him away right after the ruckus with the little girl. Didn't want to see me get in any trouble over havin' a guard dog. I've had two that I thought fer sure wouldn't hurt a flea, and here one of 'em turned out to be real vicious."

"No!" Will's protest was so vehement the screen door between them rattled with the force of it. "Buzz didn't do anything!"

"Now don't you go yellin' at me, William Winkle." Mrs. Kingston opened the door and came out onto the porch, standing nose to nose with Will. They were both the same height. "And who's this hidin' behind you?"

"Henry Higgenbotham." Henry's voice sounded small, but he spoke up immediately. "I'm Henry Higgenbotham, and we're here to ask you to reconsider your testimony against Buzz."

"There's that name agin. Who in the world is Buzz?"

"Buzzard Breath," answered Henry.

"General," said Will in the same breath, so it was hard to understand either of them.

Will started again. "The dog you got rid of—General—remember him? Well, I'm the one who adopted him from the shelter." He paused and took a deep breath before plunging ahead.

Bathsheba jumped down from Lydia Kingston's arms and made figure eights around Will's and Henry's legs, rubbing against each in turn.

"Now they're going to kill him . . . ," Will continued.

"Who's goin' to kill who?" Mrs. Kingston interrupted irritably. "I don't even know what you're talkin' about, boy."

Henry stepped forward, accidentally putting the toe of his shoe on the very tip of Bathsheba's twitching tail. The cat hissed and jumped clear, disappearing off the end of the porch.

"It's like this, Mrs. Kingston," he began in a surprisingly loud, clear voice. "The dog you knew as General—the one we call Buzz—has been framed for a crime we know he didn't commit. The people at the animal shelter are going to put him to sleep for biting the little girl who lives next door to you. But we *know* he didn't do it." Henry paused and pushed his glasses back up his sweaty nose.

"The shelter people say you were a witness to the crime, so we wanted to ask you if you could tell us *exactly* what you saw?" Henry waited a moment, then added: "Just tell us in your own words, ma'am." Like Bryan, Will thought, Henry watched too many lawyer shows on TV.

Lydia Kingston lowered herself slowly onto the porch glider. She was frowning, looking over at the freshly repainted piece of picket fencing separating her yard from her neighbor's.

"I still don't know what you boys are talkin' about. I never said anything about General to the shelter people, or to the police, neither. I told 'em about Assassin. He was the one what done the biting. I seen the whole thing. General was the one what rescued that child. He drove Assassin right away. That's all I seen. Then I went to the phone and called Howie to come over right away, and he did, too. He's a right good brother-in-law. He did most of the talkin' to the police, 'cause he knew I was all upset. And then he hauled that mean old mutt back to his farm." Lydia Kingston sighed and wrapped her arms protectively around her own chest. "Now all I've got is Alfred's baseball bat. And Bathsheba, of course."

Henry and Will were looking at each other, wide-eyed. Will broke the shocked silence with a wild Indian whoop of joy. "I *knew* Buzz didn't do it. I knew it was a mistake all along."

"Definitely a case of mistaken identity," agreed Henry in his best TV lawyer voice. But he was grinning from ear to freckled ear.

"Hurry, Mrs. Kingston." Will grabbed one of the old lady's hands. Henry grabbed the other.

Lydia Kingston snatched her hands back from the two boys. "You kids! Always in a hurry. Just keep your pants on." She began to rise slowly from the glider. "I'll go inside and give them animal shelter people a call."

"No! We have to *go* there. Their answering machine will be on at this time of day—they only pick up during business hours. We have to go now." Will's voice held a compelling note of desperation. "We have to go right now," he repeated. "Before it's too late."

"My my, how you boys go on." Lydia shook her gray pin curls in disgust, still headed for her front door.

"Please, Mrs. Kingston. Please." There was the hint of a tremble in Will's frantic plea.

Mrs. Kingston turned and looked at him. "Well, I suppose we could drive over in my car. . . ." She seemed to be thinking out loud as she opened her front door.

"Yes!" Will shouted triumphantly. "Yes! Yes!"

"Only first I have to git my car keys and my sweater and my hat, and I have to turn the stove off. . . ." Lydia Kingston ticked the items off as though she were reading them from a written list. "And, of course, I have to find Bathsheba and put her inside and put down her cat food and lock the house and . . ."

Will looked at Henry in desperation. Bathsheba could be miles away by now. Who knew how long it would take to find her?

"If you'll leave your key with me, I'll find Bathsheba and feed her," volunteered Henry. Good old Henry. Coming through again.

"Well, I don't know about that. I don't really

know you, boy, and I got a sink full of dirty dishes, and my sheets is still out on the line. . . ."

"I'll do the dishes. And fold the sheets, too. I'll do all that stuff, and I'll find Bathsheba, and then I'll lock up and leave your key under the mat." Henry had squared his shoulders and risen to his full height. Even though he was a head shorter than either Will or Mrs. Kingston, Will thought he'd never seen Henry look so tall.

A heavy, stifling silence hung in the early summer air as both boys waited for her answer. The distant noise of a siren wailing sounded loud and nearby in that silence. "Please," Will whispered, so softly he couldn't even hear the word himself. He could only feel his lips move.

"Oh, all right. If you're gonna pester me about it all afternoon, I'm not gonna be able to git anythin' done anyhow." The stillness was broken. She was getting her car keys, reaching for her hat, and giving Henry directions about how to stack the dishes in the drainer. It seemed to be taking forever, but Will knew it was just a matter of a few minutes before he was sitting beside Lydia Kingston in her thirty-year-old gray Rambler station wagon, heading for the animal shelter.

She even drove slowly. By this time Will had all his fingers crossed for luck.

"Please let us get there in time. Please let us get there in time." The words singsonged in his head, but he didn't say them out loud. Will knew that you never put good luck to the test by calling on it out loud. And he'd been lucky so far.

If you put too much weight on luck, it snaps like a rotten rope and leaves you dangling. Every kid knew that. You had to act like it didn't really matter. You had to sit on your hands and hold your breath and hope you didn't explode. Will's chest felt tight with the effort.

Lydia Kingston glanced over at him as they pulled up to their third stop light in a row. "You're gittin' all red in the face there, boy. Take a deep breath, now, and calm down. We'll be there soon enough. As my Alfred used to say to me when I was in too big a hurry, 'Where's the fire?'"

Will didn't open his mouth. He just stared straight ahead and tried not to scream. Maybe Mrs. Kingston couldn't smell the smoke, but there was a fire all right. It was burning hotly in the pit of his stomach.

Rescue

W here is he?" Will's words sounded choked. He was out of breath from running around the outside of the long concrete block building with its rows of orderly mesh pens. He'd run around it twice, searching for Buzz.

He wanted to give the dog a quick reassurance that everything was going to be okay. To tell Buzz he'd convinced Lydia Kingston to help. That as soon as the frustratingly slow old lady got her slow, clanky car locked up and finally dragged herself into the shelter's front office, she'd explain everything to the manager and Buzz would be free.

But the dog was nowhere in sight. A bug-eyed Pekingese seemed to be trying to squeeze himself through the mesh fence, barking a ridiculous high-pitched warning in the pen on one side of the empty run where Will thought Buzz should be. On the other side a gangly black-and-white-coated Labrador-mix puppy, about eight months old, with feet so big he hadn't grown into them yet, chased up and down his run, trying to invite Will to play. But Buzz's run was ominously empty.

Will hurried inside and headed straight for the office. "Where is he?" Will asked, leaning across the wide, cluttered desk until he was practically nose to nose with the shelter manager. Bertram Snavely looked up from the form he was filling out.

"Where is who?" he asked distractedly.

"My dog . . . my . . . the tan shepherd . . . the one they said bit the little girl. But he didn't . . . and he's not outside . . . I looked . . . I didn't see him. . . ." The desperation in Will's stammer seemed to get through to the man, who quietly interrupted the boy's excited explanation.

"Now, calm down, son. Oh yes. Now I remember. You're the boy who was here this morning. The kennel man told John and he told me. You wanted to prove your dog was innocent. Any luck?"

"Yes. yes! I *can* prove it! I can! My dog didn't bite anybody. I have a witness who can clear him. She's coming up the front sidewalk right now." Will strode nervously to the window and peered out between the slats of the venetian blinds. Mrs. Kingston was walking in her usual slow, deliberate way up the curving flagstone path that led to the shelter's red metal door. "See. Here she comes."

He turned back to the tall, balding man at the desk. His voice was pleading now. "But where's Buzz? Where did you move him to? He's not in the pen where you had him this morning."

"Let's just stay calm here, son," the man said soothingly. "We haven't moved any animals today, as far as I know. Of course, they don't always notify me of every little thing that goes on in the back. But I'm sure there's a simple explanation. You probably looked in the wrong pen."

Mr. Snavely stood and came around his desk with his hand extended to give Will a friendly pat on the shoulder. "I'm sure everything's fine. Why don't you and I take a walk back through the kennel area just to set your mind at ease."

He guided Will across the foyer toward the double doors that led to the back. The front door opened just then, and Lydia Kingston barged through, panting slightly as though she'd been running.

Will motioned her to follow them.

"Right through here." The shelter manager indicated the long, wide center aisle of the kennel. The cement floor was still slightly wet from its late afternoon scrub. The place smelled strongly of pine disinfectant and wet fur. And there was the lingering, sour odor of dog droppings.

Ed, the unsympathetic kennel worker from this morning, stood outside a cage at the far end of the building. Wasn't that where Buzz had been? Will began to run.

"Careful, young man. The floor's still a little wet," Mr. Snavely's voice called after him. He ran past a cage of collie-mix puppies, a white-chinned old basset hound, and a three-legged poodle. All his attention was fixed on that far-away cage. The building seemed to go out of focus, stretching longer and longer as he ran. Buzz, Buzz, please be okay.

He sprinted past the feeding alcove, where a counter stood stacked with stainless steel bowls and huge fifty-pound bags of dog food.

He pushed roughly past the man standing outside the cage. His focus was even fuzzier now. He felt as if he were watching a movie scene played out in slow motion. There was John, in white pants and a white shirt, holding Buzz between his knees. The big dog was muzzled, his body stretched upward by his captor so that he stood awkwardly on two legs, with the soft blond fur of his underbelly exposed.

A girl in a white lab coat knelt in front of him. She was aiming a needle, attached to a large syringe of yellowish fluid, at a point on Buzz's chest where she'd clipped a little clear spot in his forest of fur. Buzz whined plaintively, his tail somehow managing to thump the wall behind him as he caught sight of Will.

The veterinary technician darted the needle into the dog's chest, drawing back on the plunger of the syringe until something bright and red poured in on top of the yellowish stuff.

"I'm in the heart," the girl said, as the scene suddenly slammed out of slow motion and into fast forward. Yelling "Stop!" Will threw himself against the unlatched door of the cage, which swung forcefully into the kneeling lab tech, knocking her over. She sprawled sideways, the syringe plunger still gripped in her fingers.

Blood gushed from the unplugged syringe, still hanging in the dog's chest. It cascaded down John's white pants and onto his scuffed white tennis shoes.

"Hey! What do you think you're doing?" John started to yell, relaxing his grip on the shepherd. Buzz leaped at Will, knocking him on top of the girl in the lab coat as she struggled to get back up to a kneeling position. The open syringe hung like a swinging pendulum from the dog's chest, spraying red stuff in a stream across the clean cement floor of the pen and in a ragged stripe across the bottom of the girl's white lab coat.

Will reached up into the stickiness of Buzz's

fur with one hand, pulling out the syringe. His other arm was around the dog's neck. There were tears on his cheeks, but Buzz was nuzzling them away, his nose wet and cold through the imprisoning leather straps of his muzzle.

Lydia Kingston and Bert Snavely stood outside the cage now, looking in at the bloody spectacle. "Oh my," said Mrs. Kingston. "You were about to do the old dog in, weren't you? It's a good thing I hurried." She clucked her tongue disapprovingly. "And such a mess. Are you okay in there William Winkle? That's none of your blood, is it?"

John and the girl both sat on the floor now, looking silently at Will and the bloody mess that surrounded them. "This just isn't my day," said the girl, and both technicians started to laugh.

"I'll say," agreed John between chuckles. He reached out to give Buzz a friendly scratch between his ears. "But it *is* your day, isn't it, fella? Looks like you got a governor's stay of execution." He turned back to the girl in the white coat. "And as for you, maybe you should pack it in early and go home. After you lost that thermometer up the rectum of the big Lab mix in cage twelve, I figured that would be the worst mishap of the day. And now this. Look at my pants."

"You lost another thermometer? Is it still in the dog?" Mr. Snavely's voice, stern and accusing, brought his employees to attention.

"No, sir. Not anymore," John answered quickly. "I mean, we got it back. The dog had a stool and it came out intact."

"His temperature was normal," added the girl, and both of them began to laugh helplessly again, doubling over whenever they met each other's eyes. Even the shelter manager was smiling grudgingly.

Will unbuckled the muzzle, sliding it off the shepherd's long snout and tossing it into a corner of the cage.

"Hey, now, just a minute," Bert Snavely objected. "You're endangering my techs, young man. I'm not totally convinced yet that this animal is not a killer."

Buzz barked once, happily trailing his tongue in slurpy swipes across Will's face. As Will pushed himself up, Buzz sat obediently, looking curiously at the crowd both in and outside his cage. He looked at Mr. Snavely, thumping his tail tentatively.

"There's your 'killer,'" interrupted Mrs. Kingston. "Killer of field mice and garter snakes maybe, and even with them he'd probably rather play with the critters and leave 'em go. 'Killer,' my petunias! He's no more vicious than a butterfly. Never could make a decent guard dog out of that mutt. That's why Howie went and got me a better dog. But I never knew Howie would try a switch like this. This just don't seem fair, even if Howie is my brother-in-law."

The shelter manager took Lydia's arm and started moving her up the wide aisle. "Why don't we go back to my office, so I can get your whole statement?" As an afterthought he called over his shoulder to Will: "You can leave the muzzle off, son, but the dog has to stay in his cage until I get this cleared up. Ed, give the boy a pail and mop and let him stay with the dog and clean up that mess."

Ed nodded and hurried away.

Will knelt with his arm around Buzz, looking through the mesh at what seemed like a brand-new world. He had been so focused on Buzz that he only now noticed the chorus of barks and growls that clamored for attention throughout this end of the building. The vet tech had gotten up and left, taking her medical paraphernalia with her. Ed was coming down the aisle with a stringy mop balanced on a rolling bucket. John was curling a long orange hose around a metal holder on the wall.

"We did it, Buzz," Will whispered in the dog's ear, causing a wild tattoo of tail thumps. "You're going to be okay. I'm never going to let anybody hurt you again." He rubbed his cheek against the dog's bristly snout. "*You'd* never hurt anybody. I always knew that. You're practically a hero." He opened the gate and pulled the mop and bucket inside.

"Lie down. Down, Buzz," he commanded, and

the big dog stretched out alertly on the floor. "Now, roll over. Go ahead. Over." As the dog turned on his back, his bloody underside came into view and Will shuddered.

"You're *my* dog and nobody's ever going to hurt you again. *My* dog. *Yes.* You are." Ed had left the mop and bucket for Will to use, and now the grinning boy punctuated every sentence by swishing the dripping mop head over Buzz's blood-soaked chest fur. John had assured him that although it looked as if the dog had bled buckets, he hadn't lost enough blood to even feel dizzy. The needle-stick hole through which he'd almost gotten his fatal injection was virtually invisible. As Will mopped his dog's fur, the soapy water in the pail turned red. But Buzz's belly was fading to a cheerful pinkish tan color.

It felt good. Cool and ticklish. The boy rubbed the mop head lightly over his belly and chest, and Buzz could feel the growling moan of pleasure bubble up in his throat. It felt even better because the boy was doing it.

It had been so confusing, wearing that uncomfortable thing over his mouth and nose, and all the people holding him and poking at him. He wanted to do whatever it was they wanted him to do. But it had been impossible to tell what that was.

And then there had been all the noise.

Everyone barking warnings and the sound of urgent, running feet. Then there was the sweet, warm smell of the boy, coming closer and closer. The boy. Right there in the cage.

Buzz didn't know why the humans fell down or made the laughing noises that the boy and his friends sometimes made when they tossed him a Frisbee and he caught it. But he could feel the tension draining from the air, and he found himself dancing in circles, trying to watch everyone at the same time. He monitored the scene with his nose, especially intrigued by the pungent odor of the sticky stuff on the floor.

It had a coppery taste. He could just manage a lick through the thing over his mouth. It was salty and it made him thirsty. But when the boy took the heavy thing off his head he forgot his thirst.

He forgot everything but his master. The boy was here and he tasted like home, his smooth skin alive with the taste of everything good. Buzz licked him over and over again, stopping only when Will pushed him down and got busy with the mop.

Now the stringy mop rubbing against his stomach made Buzz's left leg twitch in a spasm of pleasure. He licked at the watery trail the soaking mop head left in his thick underfur. Despite the soapiness, it tasted good. It tasted like the cool tile on the bathroom floor at home.

Buzz knew he wasn't home yet. But the boy was right here beside him.

And wherever the boy was, that meant home to Buzz.

Epilogue

What do you call him?" asked a young man, kneeling down to scratch under the big shepherd's chin.

Will and Buzz were waiting to go up on stage. It was award time at the annual Humane Society banquet, and Buzz was getting a medal for his part in the rescue of little Anita Adams, the two-year-old he'd saved from Assassin's cowardly attack.

After Howard Kingston confessed the whole story, Assassin was taken to the pound for rabies testing. The black dog's future was uncertain, but at least the puppy farm, where Howard had treated his dog stock so cruelly, had been closed down by the state for health violations.

"His name is Buzzard Breath." Will said the

words proudly. He knew now what his mother meant when she said, "Name something, and it's yours forever."

"Funny name for a fighter." The young man wore a camouflage jacket, torn blue jeans, and a gold hoop in his left ear. "But I bet he'd make quite a guard dog."

Will didn't answer. Lydia Kingston, who was sitting at the table on Will's right, laughed out loud. "Samson here's a better guard dog than that soft-hearted fool," she said to Will's mother, who was seated beside her. "I do want you to know how much I appreciate your family's help in finding this little angel for me, Mrs. Winkle. I believe I've finally got it right."

Mrs. Kingston was stroking a flat-faced Pekingese, who was seated alertly on her lap. At first glance Samson looked almost like a twin to Bathsheba. He was the same creamy color, with the same long, silken hair, and the same pushed-in nose. But Samson, whom Will had seen that last day at the shelter, was 100 percent dog.

He adored his new mistress. He barked—a high-pitched, almost comical sound—at anything that came close. He'd even chased the postman once, hanging on ferociously to the cuff of the man's pants leg as the mail carrier tried to shake him off. He was the perfect dog for Lydia Kingston.

Henry, who sat on the other side of Will, with Max in his lap, leaned over and spoke softly in

Will's ear. "I'm just glad Samson likes *us*," he whispered with a giggle. "Since we're over there every Saturday." Will nodded, thinking how great it was that Mrs. Kingston had hired Henry to help him with the yard work. She'd even decided to pay Will for his time, now that he'd worked off the repairs to her porch.

"Listen, I might be interested in buying this dog," continued the young man with the earring. "I'm starting a business, and I need a strong, intelligent animal to patrol the grounds. This one looks like he'd fill the bill just fine."

"He's not for sale." Will answered quickly, and as soon as the words dropped off his tongue he knew they sounded familiar. Of course! It was that line from *The Proud Rebel.* Will could hear the movie dialogue playing in his head: "How much do ya want for that dog a yourn, son?"

He'd already answered the man once, but now he said the words again, liking the loud, proud sound of them. "He's not for sale at any price, mister." Buzz thumped his tail against Will's leg and barked his agreement.

A voice boomed over the microphone: "Will Winkle and Buzzard Breath, to the stage please." There were a few giggles and some low whispering in the audience as boy and dog headed to the front of the room.

"Ah! So this is the dog with the unusual name!" exclaimed the emcee when they reached the stage.

Buzz's picture had been in the newspaper the day before, with a caption under it explaining what he'd done and giving his name. When they'd gone out to deliver today, five separate people had stopped Will to ask if he'd seen the picture. He had, of course. His dad had bought a dozen copies.

The emcee bent over in his tuxedo to pet Buzz, and the microphone pinned to his lapel gave an electric shriek of protest. But the dog ignored him, looking intently up into Will's face. It was as if the rest of the world didn't even exist.

"So, tell us, son. Did the paper get it right? Just what is the official name of this magnificent animal?" asked the announcer, unhooking his mike and passing it over to Will.

"This is Winkle's Warrior Buzzard Breath of Notchcliff," said Will in a clear, firm voice. "But his friends just call him Buzz."

The applause grew loud as Will looked out over the audience, full of dogs and people. Will wondered if he was really hearing bells ringing, or if it was just his imagination. He could see registered dalmatians, blue-ribbon poodles, and exotic bichon frises. They were all good dogs, but they weren't for him.

Will didn't care about money or papers. He didn't care about class or breeding. He just cared about Buzz.

The perfect dog was one thing. But Buzzard Breath was his best friend.